GLIMPSE

When Jeffrey Collins stops his car to help an injured motorcyclist, the hurt man vanishes before his eyes! Collins approaches a scientist, Dr. Whittaker, for an explanation. But when Whittaker is found dead from poisoning, Collins is accused of murder. The evidence against him is damning: he'd quarrelled with Whittaker, and they both stood to make a fortune from some kind of formula. Collins, unable to explain, is found guilty — and so begins an astounding odyssey of space, time, and destiny.

JOHN RUSSELL FEARN

GLIMPSE

Complete and Unabridged

LINFORD
Leicester

First published in Great Britain

First Linford Edition
published 2010

British Library CIP Data

Fearn, John Russell, *1908 – 1960.*
    Glimpse.- -(Linford mystery library)
    1. Poisoning- -Fiction. 2. Scientists- -
    Crimes against- -Fiction. 3. Judicial error- -
    Fiction. 4. Detective and mystery stories.
    5. Large type books.
    I. Title II. Series
    823.9′12–dc22

    ISBN 978–1–44480–343–3

Published by
F. A. Thorpe (Publishing)
Anstey, Leicestershire

Set by Words & Graphics Ltd.
Anstey, Leicestershire
Printed and bound in Great Britain by
T. J. International Ltd., Padstow, Cornwall

This book is printed on acid-free paper

1

The man who vanished

Jeffrey Collins was feeling well satisfied with himself. He was a 'commercial' and had had a particularly good day. Things had been pretty slack lately, and Betty had been complaining that there was not nearly enough money coming in — but the next commission cheque ought to show a difference. Like most newly-married young couples, the Collins' needed every penny they could get if they were to build up a background for the future.

Jeffrey Collins felt pleased enough to start whistling as he drove his noisy little car towards Marbrook, the small town to the north of Birmingham where his home lay.

It was a nasty November night with a sou'wester howling across the fields and rain swilling down the car's windscreen. It was even leaking through the roof into Jeffrey's lap. Not that he cared. Soft hat on the back of his head, raincoat collar turned up around his ears, he drove on steadily, the wiper cutting a flawless segment in the raindrops reflecting prismatically the glare from his headlights.

Then Jeffrey saw it. At first he thought it was a motorcycle that had broken down and that the rider was trying to repair it. His mind full of the code of the highway, Jeffrey pulled up as his headlights illuminated the stranger — but even as he put on the brakes Jeffrey was aware of something remarkable. The machine that had broken down was not a motorcycle, and the rider was a remarkable figure.

He wore scarcely any clothes and what little there were seemed limited to tight golden trunks that had an amazing sheen in the light, and a kind of breastplate of metal. Otherwise, except for sandals, the man was naked, a magnificently muscled giant well over six feet and with the face of a Greek god.

Jeffrey lowered the car window. 'Having trouble?' he asked, and tried to recall if there was a fancy dress ball on anywhere around here.

Then the man turned, and Jeffrey received a shock. Until now he had only seen him three-quarter face. Now he saw it fully he noticed a frightful gash on the man's left temple, blood streaming from it.

'Mirani haj kilmo ni juson,' the man said, gripping his wounded head and swaying dangerously.

'Oh!' Jeffrey opened his mouth and then shut it. He was no linguist, but he did know he had not heard any recognisable foreign language. It was sheer gibberish.

'I'm Jeffrey Collins,' he resumed, climbing out into the rain. 'You need a doctor, or the hospital. What happened?'

He looked more closely at the man's machine. It was a strange affair of shining bars, glass brackets, and tubes that connected with two ground supports rather like skis. There was also a big saddle.

'Linhaj mio tif gulio,' the giant said vaguely.

'I don't get it!' Jeffrey said. 'Either

you're nuts or I am. Fact remains, you need help. Give me a hand and I'll cart this bike of yours along.'

The giant plainly did not understand the words, but he grasped the significance of Jeffrey's actions. He lifted the strange 'vehicle' in his mighty arms and carried it to the back of the car. Jeffrey pulled open the boot and the giant heaved the machine on to the shelf.

Jeffrey opened the car door and they got in. Once they were inside the giant was so huge that Jeffrey had difficulty in fitting him into his seat. He was intent on reaching the Marbrook General Hospital as quickly as possible, because he was convinced that the giant was bleeding to death.

Jeffrey started the car and asked hesitantly: 'Can you understand what I am saying?'

The giant, holding his bleeding temple, looked at him but did not answer. In the dim dashboard light Jeffrey glimpsed the magnificent features, the thick blond hair, the mighty muscles — and then he had gone.

Just like that! Jeffrey found himself

staring at an empty seat with the dark rectangle of the car window beyond.

Mechanically he stopped the car. He couldn't have dreamed it all. No! His cigarette lighter flame held near the floor showed the still-wet bloodstains, and they were spattered on the leather seat, too.

Jeffrey did the only thing he could, once he had partially recovered from the shock. He drove home — and the first thing his wife Betty noticed was the dazed look in his eyes.

'What's the matter with you?' she asked. 'Had another bad day, I suppose?'

With an effort Jeffrey came back to earth. 'Bad? No. A good one. Almost a thousand pounds' worth of commission.'

'A thousand?' Betty's eyes went wide, then all of a sudden she was the smiling girl Jeffrey had married. She flung her arms around his neck and kissed him, then with her dark hair bobbing about her shoulders she led the way into the living room.

'Everything's ready,' she said and went into the kitchen.

Jeffrey sat down by the fire and stared into it.

'Come on,' Betty complained presently. 'The stew's ready and I'm hungry. And I'm sure you must be.'

'Sorry, Bet.' Jeffrey started. 'I was miles away.'

'So it seems. Though I can forgive you when I think of the thousand pounds commission.'

Jeffrey took his seat at the table but did not seem to see the food put before him. His brows knitted, he was staring at the artificial flowers in the bowl in the centre of the table. Betty waited impatiently, studying his intelligent features, abstracted grey eyes and untidy fair hair. In the ordinary way Jeffrey was not a bad-looking fellow, but at the moment he was clearly in some kind of a daze.

'What is it?' Betty demanded. 'Or don't you like the flowers?'

Jeffrey only nodded and ate his stew mechanically, still looking into space. He had a vague idea that Betty still chattered on, covering various irrelevant subjects, then he said suddenly: 'I've got to tell

6

somebody — though I'll be darned if I know what.'

'Tell somebody? About what?' Betty stared at him.

'About a godlike man I picked up tonight who vanished into thin air while he sat beside me. He was terribly injured and there's blood in the car to prove it. And some sort of a bicycle. That's in the back of the car.'

'What on earth are you talking about?' Betty demanded.

Jeffrey got to his feet. 'Slip a coat on and come into the garage. I'll show you.'

Bewildered, Betty obeyed. With a torch in his hand and coat thrown over his shoulders Jeffrey led the way across the yard. In the garage he switched on the light and yanked open the car door. Betty peered inside and gave a little gasp when she saw the bloodstains. Not all of them were dry yet.

'What does it mean?' she asked in bewilderment. 'You — you didn't kill somebody, did you?'

'Of course I didn't! I tell you there was a man who . . . ' Jeffrey then gave the

7

whole story. She stared at him throughout and finally looked about her as though she expected a half-naked man to materialize at any moment.

'And look at his machine,' Jeffrey said, then led the way round to the back of the car and tried to move the queer machine.

'I can't budge it. Yet that chap carried it as though it were a fairy-cycle. And with his head half bashed in at that.'

Betty was looking at the machine.

'What on earth is this?' she said. 'It doesn't resemble anything I ever saw before.'

'Nor I. Now do you see why I've got to tell somebody? I must. This mystery's driving me crazy. Seems to me it's a scientific problem.'

Betty only nodded, because anything that smelled of science made her wish to yawn immediately.

'Old Doc Whittaker doesn't live far from here,' Jeffrey continued, thinking. 'I know he's a scientist because he's always writing articles for the papers about atoms and the future of mankind. Maybe he'd be interested in this lot.'

Betty merely shrugged. 'Anyway, now we've seen the bloodstains and this thing, there's nothing more we can do without an explanation from somebody. And I didn't finish my meal, either.'

'Okay. Later I'll have to clean the inside of the car.'

His mind made up Jeffrey followed her back into the house and picked up the telephone.

After he had rang the doctor's number a gruff voice answered: 'Dr. Whittaker speaking.'

Jeffrey introduced himself, then said: 'I have a problem at my house in which I think you might be interested.'

'Why should I be?'

'Please, Dr. Whittaker. Listen!'

Jeffrey proceeded to give the whole story, and Dr. Whittaker said: 'You sound sober, young man — and I know you are young by your voice. Probably the foolish type but not necessarily imaginative. I'll admit you have aroused my curiosity. How do I get to your place?'

'My home is Forty-two Pine Crescent, about ten minutes from your place. I'll bring the car if you like, though it's pretty badly stained inside.'

'Leave the car where it is, young man, and the vehicle on the back of it. I'll be with you in fifteen minutes.'

Satisfied, Jeffrey rang off. He hung up his mackintosh again and returned to his meal. Betty was nearly at the end of hers and she gave him a questioning look.

'What's Dr. Whittaker going to do?'

'Coming over in about fifteen minutes which gives me time to finish this meal and freshen up a bit. He sounds a queer sort of egg. Either bad-tempered or eccentric or both.'

It was still a puzzle to know which when he came using a car which for some unexplained reason made no noise at all. Presumably Dr. Whittaker was a man with ideas of his own.

In appearance he was vaguely dominating. He was over six feet tall, very thin, and wearing baggy tweeds. Iron grey hair sprouted from a large head. He fixed Betty with piercing eyes as she stood in the hall beside him, not quite sure what to do.

'Mmm — Mrs. — er — I suppose.' Whittaker looked vague. 'I wasn't given the name on the 'phone.'

'My fault, Doctor,' Jeffrey apologized, hurrying down the stairs. 'I'm Jeffrey Collins. This is my wife Betty.'

Introductions over, Whittaker asked briefly: 'Where is it?'

'Out here — ' Jeffrey snatched down his raincoat and led the way outside with Whittaker striding after him. Betty hesitated for a moment, then not to be outdone, followed in a roughly draped mackintosh.

Jeffrey indicated the strange machine on the back of the car.

'Mmm . . . ' This was Dr. Whittaker's only immediate comment.

'It isn't like any machine you'd see in the ordinary way, is it?' Jeffrey asked.

'No. And what about the bloodstains you mentioned?'

For several minutes Whittaker studied them in the torchlight, then he straightened up, a profound look of interest upon his lean features.

'You haven't shown anybody else these

stains?' he questioned, and Jeffrey shook his head.

'I'm not asking for trouble like that. If I told the police they belonged to a man who mysteriously disappeared, I'd be accused of murder or something.'

'I see your point.' Whittaker looked absently around the garage and then he said: 'You have hit upon something of extreme value, young man, though I hardly expect you to be aware how valuable. I want you to sell me this car — intact, just as it is. You can name your own price.'

'Sell it to you?' Jeffrey looked blank. 'But why?'

'I wish to examine these bloodstains at my leisure and with technical apparatus. I cannot do it by just scraping away the deposit when it is dry. Besides, I may need quite a lot of them to make my tests. Bloodstains, in case you don't know it, play an enormous part in determining heredity and so forth.'

'Yes, I suppose so. I've heard of things like that. And what about that old iron on the back? Do you want that as well?'

'Definitely. Include it in the price for the car.'

Jeffrey pondered; then Betty nudged him and whispered: 'We need money and he can afford to throw it about. Lay it on thick.'

Jeffrey gave her a reproving glance and cleared his throat. 'How about twenty thousand pounds?'

'Right!' Whittaker agreed, without hesitation, and tugged out his cheque-book. 'Being a dark night, I can risk driving it home without the ownership and so forth being transferred. We can fix that later. I'll return for my own car later, too . . . Your cheque, Mr. Collins. From here on, everything about this car is mine. Understood?'

'Of course. Good night, Doctor.' Jeffrey took the cheque and looked at it, then as Whittaker began to settle into the driving seat, Betty moved forward.

'But just a moment, Dr. Whittaker. Don't we ever get to know what this mystery's all about? Don't we know what — '

'Of course, of course,' Whittaker

interrupted impatiently. You know my address. Drop in from time to time, and whatever I have discovered I will pass on to you.'

'Fair enough,' Jeffrey agreed, and opened the garage doors. 'And I'll fix the transfer of ownership first thing in the morning.'

Whittaker nodded and started up the engine, then he said: 'As I said, I'll be back shortly for my own car. Don't try to move it. It works by a new propulsion system entirely my own.'

Jeffrey and Betty looked at each other in wonder and Dr. Whittaker drove away.

Disappointed for a moment Betty watched Whittaker disappearing, then she returned into the house with Jeffrey close behind her. And, suddenly, her mood changed.

'Twenty thousand pounds, Jeff, for practically nothing!' she exclaimed, hugging him. 'This must be our lucky day — and coming right on top of your big commission, too!'

'Not exactly for nothing,' Jeffrey said. 'No man pays twenty thousand so easily as that without mighty good reason. I must have blundered into something far more valuable than I thought. And anyway the cheque isn't clear profit. I have to buy another car.'

'You can buy another car and still have plenty left over.'

Jeffrey was silent, deep in speculation . . . In the back of his mind he was far from satisfied. Why had Whittaker reminded him that everything about the car had been transferred to him? What had he really stumbled into? At the earliest moment he meant to find out.

The following day — after Whittaker had called for his own strange car and had nothing particular to say — Jeffrey made the legal transfer arrangements, looked over another car for himself, and for a fortnight afterwards continued his normal business; but all the time he was haunted by the mystery that had come into his life and disappeared again. Finally he could stand it no longer and detoured on his way home one evening to see if Whittaker was willing to volunteer any information.

He found the doctor as matter-of-fact as ever, attired in a somewhat tattered smock, and apparently alone in his big house.

'Come into the laboratory,' he invited briefly. 'I'm extremely busy. This way . . . '

Jeffrey found himself directed through a long passageway and finally into a brightly lighted annex to the house. In the centre of the floor stood the weird vehicle that had formerly been fastened to the car. Just how it had been moved this far Jeffrey did not dare to question.

'Naturally,' Whittaker said, considering a foaming test tube, 'you've come to find out if I've discovered anything?'

'Correct — and you can't blame me for that. Have you found anything?'

'I have. For the past few weeks I've been conducting very exhaustive blood tests on those stains. Here you see the result . . . '

Jeffrey looked at the various phials in the racks, each of them containing curious liquids and scummy sediments.

'I started with the benzedrine test,' Whittaker went on, 'and after that I

16

worked my way through Groups and Plasma Basis to an answer. You see, in regard to blood, you can tell the age of a person, the approximate point in the scale of evolution, and the particular group. That is O, A, B, or AB. Following this I went through the Group Incidence and then carried out tests with the Agglutinogens M and N to test heredity — And you don't know what in hell I'm talking about, do you?'

'It isn't very clear,' Jeffrey admitted mildly.

'I'll make it plainer. Heredity and race can be traced by a particular type of blood, and the man you picked up does not — or did not — belong to any group which exists within measurable time since records were kept.'

'Then — then where does he fit in?'

'Dim antiquity, young man. Dim antiquity.'

'But that's idiotic! How could a man from dim antiquity have a machine like that?'

Whittaker brooded for a moment. 'The ancients were much cleverer than we are,

17

Mr. Collins. That is freely admitted.'

'So I've heard, but what's that got to do with me picking up a man on a country road in twenty twelve?'

Whittaker smiled inscrutably. 'That object in the middle of the floor there, which you mistook for something as ordinary as a motorcycle, Mr. Collins, is a time machine.'

Jeffrey looked at it, thoughts of H. G. Wells chasing through his brain. Then Whittaker continued speaking.

'My analysis of the blood traces shows that racially the man concerned dates back an incredible length of time,' Whittaker resumed. 'Dating back, indeed, to a race which has no existence in the world today. I speculated on the possibility of the man having to come from the future to the present time, but had that been so — no matter how far in the future his starting point might have been — there would have been traces in his blood plasma of certain elements present in the groups of today. Since there were none I am led to the inescapable belief that he came from the past into what, to him, was the future. To us it is the present.'

'But what of the past?' Jeffrey asked. 'There were only apes, savages, and — lowest of all — amoeba.'

'You have overlooked the great civilizations which vanished through causes we have never satisfactorily explained. Atlantis leaps to the mind. Atlantis of Mu. It is generally conceded that the scientists of that city were infinitely cleverer than the scientists of today. A time machine sent from there might easily have reached here.'

'Are you certain that that thing there is a time machine?'

Whittaker looked impatient. 'Not yet. I've just been telling you: I'm tracing by blood groups. If the man came from the past then only that machine could have brought him. That's logical enough, isn't it?'

'I suppose it is. But why did he vanish so suddenly?'

'I think the only answer to that is to get this machine to work and go back in Time and find the solution — which is what I intend doing. If I can succeed in travelling in Time I shall be the greatest scientist in the world — which is what I deserve with a long series of accomplishments in other fields behind me.'

'Which is why you bought everything for twenty thousand?' Jeffrey asked.

Whittaker shrugged. 'I realized the possibilities. It was worth twenty thousand to me to try and make a mighty discovery. Though you have no claim in this I'm quite willing to tell you what I discover.'

'Suppose,' Jeffrey asked slowly, 'I don't let you get away with it quite like that?'

'With what?'

'If you travel Time backwards and make yourself famous because of it, I demand a share. Partnership if you like. I found the man.'

'And you sold everything to me.'

'I did, without realizing what I was doing. But if anything comes of your investigation I demand equal limelight. Besides, I'm in need of money.'

'I noticed you have an extravagant wife. It's written all over her. You always find it with those full faces and dimpled chins. Such types date back to the — '

'Never mind that! What about cutting me in for half of the glory?'

'No,' Whittaker said. 'If you expect me to share the plaudits of science with a commercial traveller, Mr. Collins, you're vastly mistaken!'

'Very well,' Jeffrey said grimly. 'If anything comes of this I'll advertise it to the world that I discovered the original time traveller.'

'If you wish — but legally you have no claim.'

Jeffrey drove away from the house in a bitter mood. Whittaker was left undisturbed. Dismissing Jeffrey Collins from his mind he moved to the time machine and studied it.

He found the contrivance singularly baffling in design, and because there was no other way to discover anything than by trial and error he began to experiment, as he had done several times recently, with the various switches on the small control panel. To do it he seated himself in the big saddle with its powerful springs, his feet in specially-contrived rests.

He moved a switch he had not tried before — and something happened. At which time Jeffrey Collins had returned home and was striding into the room to discover that Betty had just got a meal together after being out most of the day.

'You're early,' she announced, peeved.

'On the contrary, I'm late. You've been gadding around, I suppose, on that shopping money you asked for?'

'I've got to have some kind of a change, haven't I? I can't stick in here all day just waiting for you ... And I don't believe you are late. You're just saying it.'

'I tell you I am. I stopped to have a word with Dr. Whittaker and it took a good ten minutes.'

'Oh. How's he making out?'

'He expects to make a fortune out of that contraption I had on the back of the car.'

'A fortune?' Betty's expression changed. 'Then why on earth did you let him get away with it like that? And you let it go for a miserable twenty thousand!'

'You stampeded me into that. He's

discovered something that will make him famous. That mystery man I picked up came from a remote period in the past, probably the time of Atlantis.'

'Where?' Betty looked vacant.

'Skip it,' Jeffrey sighed. 'You wouldn't understand. What about tea?'

'It's ready,' she snapped.

He settled at the table to begin his meal, but he had hardly commenced before the front door bell rang. He went out into the hall, switching on the light, and opened the front door — then he stepped back in amazement. Framed against the blackness of the night was a most extraordinary figure — shaggy, his clothes in rags, a beard halfway to his chest.

'Don't stand there gawping!' barked the voice of Dr. Whittaker. 'Invite me in, can't you?'

'Eh? Oh, of course.' Jeffrey could hardly find words. He was too overcome with shock. He motioned and the unkempt scientist entered.

'What's the idea of the fancy dress, Dr. Whittaker?'

'This hair and beard are genuine!' Whittaker retorted. 'And these rags and tatters are the remains of the suit you saw me in earlier this evening. I've been away three months. And what a three months!'

In the living room Whittaker dropped wearily into the nearest armchair. Betty started, her mouth open, then at Jeffrey's signal she poured out some tea quickly. Whittaker took the cup and seemed to revive a little.

'Thanks,' he muttered. Then: 'Considering the uneasy terms on which we parted this evening, Mr. Collins, you must be wondering why I've come here looking like this.'

'That's an understatement. I can't see how you've been away three months when it can't be above an hour since we parted from each other.'

'Time ratio,' Whittaker said, staring fixedly before him for a moment; then he seemed to get a better grip on himself. 'You happened to be the nearest person I could think of,' he explained. 'It was even more to the point my coming here because you know exactly how I looked an hour ago. Yet look now — pull this hair and beard . . . Go on! Genuine!'

Jeffrey obeyed and looked more startled than ever.

'I've been back through Time,' Whittaker explained. 'It happened before I realized it. I was experimenting with the switches on that contraption and one of them worked. I found myself hurtling through sub-space with a maze of transformations shuttling around me. How long it actually took I don't know. It seemed hours, but couldn't have been more than seconds — as we understand time. I came here to tell you everything. You'll believe it, remembering me as I was an hour ago.'

Jeffrey poured out more tea and solemnly handed it over.

'To cut matters short,' Whittaker said, 'I found myself in Atlantis — and I mean the Atlantis which existed before catastrophe overtook it and plunged it to the bottom of the ocean. I found it prosperous, thriving and I was able to exchange information because some kind of brain-vibration machine was used on me, which made me able to understand the language. I was pumped dry of information and I learnt, incidentally, what happened to your strange friend.'

'You did?' Jeffrey tensed forward eagerly.

'He made the Time trip from his own Time to ours for an experiment. He could have selected any future period of course, but it happened he chose ours. By a complicated process he was linked through the Time-curvature — as the Atlanteans call it — by a magnetic force that reacted shortly after his machine had finished its trip. Because of that he was dissolved into his atomic constituents and reassembled again in his own Time. I saw him, quite recovered from his injury . . . '

Whittaker became silent again. Betty gave Jeffrey a dumbfounded look and waited, sat like an image.

'Funny thing,' Whittaker resumed, 'but all the time I was in Atlantis I never saw a woman. Either there were none or else they were kept in constant subjection. There is also another possibility — that all women in that Age were extinct for some reason, which would account for the later disappearance of the Atlanteans, there being no progeny . . . '

'Anyway I was pumped dry of information by the city dignitaries; then being allowed to wander as I chose I picked up some secrets, one of them being a formula to neutralise old age. I also discovered that the time machine had had its control bar set at Atlantean time, so with its forward journey finished there was nothing it could do, when reversed, but go back where it had come. The man you saw was apparently only making adjustments.'

'With that injury!' Jeffrey gasped.

'The Atlanteans make light of injury. They have complete mastery of matter — I mean had. I keep speaking in the present tense because I can't see it any other way. I know you must believe everything I say because I'm here as living evidence.'

Jeffrey's eyes strayed over Whittaker's ragged appearance and mane of flowing hair. He looked older — much older.

'How could you live three months in

one hour?' Betty demanded.

'Time, Mrs. Collins, is purely an arbitrary term,' Whittaker replied. 'The only way we can measure time is by clocks and watches, the movement of the sun and planets, the period taken by any object to cover a certain amount of space. It is not a tangible thing. Had we been educated to believe that a second occupies as much time as a minute we would believe it. It is not a fixed thing. It can be proven by the fact that if we are anxious for something to develop, ten seconds can seem like ten minutes. On the other hand, if we are enjoying something and wish the time to last we find an hour has disappeared in what seems only a few minutes. It's a state of consciousness, madam. And very important.'

Betty gave a weak smile and let the matter drop.

'I was in Atlantis three months by their calendar,' Whittaker stated, 'yet when I got back here I discovered only an hour had elapsed. The cause can only be a different state of consciousness in a Time removed from our own. Certainly it was at least three months or I could not have grown all this!'

'Don't those other people shave?' Betty asked.

'They have no need. Their faces are hairless. I was considered a throwback — a throwback from the future! Maybe they were right since my intellect did not equal theirs. I just let my hair and beard grow and poked around all I could. Then I realized that sticking there and being fed, housed, and secretly watched was no use to me. I had to make an effort to get back home. I knew where the machine had been put — the one in which I had reached Atlantis. It was just a matter of circumventing the guards. In the interval I had found out how to set the machine's guiding pointer to whatever Time might be needed. When the chance came I acted. I'm a pretty big man, and strong, and I caught the guards by surprise. Before they could do anything I was on the machine, whipped the pointer over to my own Time, and — here I am.'

'And suppose,' Jeffrey asked, musing, 'some of these Atlanteans come into the future — as it is to them — looking for you?'

Whittaker shrugged. 'Why should they? I'm a no-account specimen from their point of view, so I hardly think they'd take that much trouble.'

'Why,' Jeffrey asked, 'do you tell me all this? We parted on pretty cool terms, Dr. Whittaker. You could have kept all this to yourself.'

'I could, but what good would it have done me? When I relate this adventure to a scientific conclave I want you as a witness — with my hair and beard as guarantee.'

'Yes,' Jeffrey agreed. 'I suppose they are that. What happens now?'

Whittaker, evidently recovered now from his exhausting experience, rose from his chair and began to pace the small room. After a moment or two of reflection he halted and said:

'Earlier I was determined to keep everything to myself, so I told you when you came to see me — but the way things have worked out I am going to need you as a witness when I explain things to the scientific profession. So I am cutting you in as a partner after all. Forgive my earlier avarice, if you can.'

Jeffrey considered for a while, then he nodded. 'Very well. I'm a partner, and I want it legal. Fifty-fifty in whatever might accrue from all this.'

'I'm willing. This thing is too big for one man to handle — not just the Time business, which is a profound problem for the scientists to work on, but the defeat of old age. Do you realize the profit that can be made out of an idea like this?'

'If it works,' Jeffrey commented dubiously, and Whittaker glared at him.

'I'm talking of a formula devised by the cleverest scientists who ever lived! The Atlanteans! They use it to give themselves a life span of something like five to seven thousand years. Therein lies — or did lie — their greatness.'

'But,' Betty put in, 'if they can move up and down in Time, why need they spread their lives for seven thousand years?'

Whittaker retorted: 'To be able to move seven thousand years onwards in Time does not accomplish anything. You merely see things as they will be seven thousand years hence. But to build up a mighty civilization you must live through every moment of that seven thousand years, moulding, devising, planning ... You understand?'

'No,' Betty answered, lowering her eyes.

Whittaker looked for a moment as though he were going to say what he really thought about the female of the species, but he controlled himself.

He turned to Jeffrey and said: 'I shall have need of you as a witness many times, so can we shake hands on that?'

'And sign a legal document agreeing to partnership?' Jeffrey insisted.

'Certainly! Tomorrow if you like. After that we will work out some kind of plan between us. That neutralizer for old age can make us fabulously wealthy. If it were that alone, I would keep it to myself, but if I did I would have to forego telling the Science Association about Time travel, because without you, and your wife, to state on oath how I came here tonight and how I looked, I would not be believed. It is settled, Mr. Collins. We are partners.'

Jeffrey shook hands and smiled. He felt that for the first time he really understood Dr. Irwin Whittaker.

★ ★ ★

The next day Irwin Whittaker had the deed of partnership drawn up by a reputable lawyer, and he and Jeffrey signed it. This being done Whittaker made a video film of himself, after which he felt safe to get a shave and haircut. Jeffrey took care of a few local calls and visited Whittaker again in the evening.

'Glad you came,' Whittaker said, looking his normal self. 'I've contacted the Scientific Association and they have convened a meeting specially to hear of my Time experience and to see the machine. I also want you to see the formula for old age neutralisation.'

In the laboratory Jeffrey found himself looking again at that queer contraption which could move into past or future.

'Did you discover how it does it, Doc?' he asked.

'No, I didn't find out the complete secret. If I had I'd be master of the world. I learned smatterings, though. It seems it causes a curvature in the dimension we loosely call space. We cannot move in Time without moving in space; but this machine renders space negative so that only the Time dimension functions. Thereby you move in Time without moving in space. Stop the action of space and you're free to move into either past or future without the added impediment of space. Clear?'

'No, but I dimly see what you mean.'

'There is a simile,' Whittaker added. 'Have you not sat in a train and seen another train next to you start moving away? Have you not been sure for the moment that your train was on the move — until a glance through the opposite window at the stationary platform changes your view? This machine acts like that. When space is halted the machine is motionless but the Dimension of Time continues to pass by it. Maybe we'll learn more about it later. For the moment I want to explain this old age neutralisation formula to you. Come over here, please.'

With a final longing glance at the time machine, Jeffrey did as he ordered, feeling rather like a schoolboy in the toils of an irate physics master. But inwardly he had come to like Irwin Whittaker quite a lot now their first misunderstanding had been cleared up. There was a rugged bluntness about the man, which lifted him out of the ordinary rut.

Whittaker indicated a mass of figures on a scratchpad. 'These are my notes just as I made them in Atlantis: though it belongs to a past time, the ingredients are present in past, present, and future, so it is operative. As to the formula itself, old age is caused by the slow breakdown, throughout life, of the cells forming the body. A process called ketabolism. The opposite process is anabolism — building-up. It would appear from this formula that a certain combination of chemicals, all obtainable in this day and age, thank heaven, can stop the effect of ketabolism and indefinitely hold it at bay. There is a limit of about ten thousand years. Think of that as a marketable product, young man! Old age abolished! What will people not pay for such a gift?'

'I still say *if it* works. And how can you find out? We can't try it on somebody and wait about five thousand years or so to see if it works!'

'That's just what we are going to do,' Whittaker said. 'And I can trust you because you are in on this as much as I am.'

Jeffrey glanced quickly towards the time machine.

'You — you mean — ?' He stopped, his eyes wide.

'I mean you or I — preferably you — can try some of this drug,' Whittaker explained. 'If you don't wish to, then I will. It's immaterial. One of us will go five thousand years into the future to see if you, or I, whichever takes the drug, is still alive and active. Or the records of that time, if there are any, will perhaps give the answer.'

'It won't be an easy job,' Jeffrey commented. 'In the course of five thousand years you, or I, might be anywhere. It might take heaven knows how long to make contact. It is hardly likely you will be exactly on this spot, is it?'

'Hardly,' Whittaker admitted. 'As an instance of that when I returned to this Time I found myself half a mile from here which is just the distance the Atlanteans moved the machine in their Time. So, of course, in the future we are bound to move in space as well as in Time. However, I don't think it ought to prove so difficult to make contact for any man who has lived five thousand years will inevitably be dominating the world.'

After watching Whittaker mix the ingredients of the strange drug Jeffrey said: 'I can't be the one to take the drug. I have responsibilities — my wife, for instance. It wouldn't be fair to her to involve myself in risks.'

Whittaker shrugged. 'Very well. I will take it and you will travel Time. Things being in the ratio they are you should find out all you need within an hour of normal time, though it may be apparently weeks to you whilst you are in the future.'

'You are perfectly sure you know how to make this machine travel futurewards? I mean — there won't be some kind of fault, which might strand me between one Time and the other?'

'Definitely not. The method is infallible.' Whittaker abandoned his drug mixing for a moment and crossed to the time machine. He indicated a metal pointer fixed to a delicate spindle. 'The pointer's tip is designed to sweep across a semicircle of numbers marked in hundreds up to 10,000, with hairlines between,' he explained.

Jeffrey peered dubiously at the markings. 'I can't recognize any of the numbers,' he remarked.

'That's because they're in Atlantean symbols. But their system of mathematics was the same as ours. These groupings of numbers are in thousands. All you need recognize is the zero symbol here — ' he indicated it. 'That zero number belongs to Atlantis itself. And our own time is — here. If we advance the pointer across five groupings from now that will cover five thousand years into the future.' He made the advancement. 'The machine will finish operating when that distance through Time has been covered. The power is sub-atomic and no immediate concern of yours. As I explained, all it does is affect space around you not moving in itself by a fraction of an inch. This is the actuating lever.'

Jeffrey looked at it uneasily, then at the big saddle.

'If anything goes wrong and I *forget* how get back, what do I do?'

'There's an automatic change-back device here which will operate if you wish to return without setting the controls. By and large, the apparatus is foolproof. The only thing is: have you the nerve to make the trip? *Or* do you prefer to take the drug and let me make the journey? I've had some experience along that line, remember.'

'I'll risk it. How long will you be finishing that drug?'

'About ten minutes.'

Whittaker returned to the bench, but his estimate proved optimistic. It was an hour and a half before the formula was completed. The result was an emerald green oily fluid.

'Elixir of the gods!' he murmured, holding it to the light. 'Seems no reason to use injection, so here goes.'

He hesitated for a moment, then drank the liquid at a gulp and put the tall glass back on the bench.

'That's that,' he said quietly, considering the formula again. 'I included everything, and, as far as it is humanly possible to be correct, I did not omit anything. The rest is up to you, Mr. Collins.'

Jeffrey glanced at the clock. It was just 7.30. He particularly wanted to know the time so that he could check up when he came back. He moved to the machine and clambered gingerly to the saddle. Following Whittaker's directions he put his feet on the rests.

'Okay?' Whittaker questioned.

'Near as can be . . .' For a moment Jeffrey was haunted by the thought that maybe he had walked into a trap and that Whittaker had planned some scheme to be completely rid of him. Well, supposing this were so, what was the answer? To accuse him openly of such subterfuge was impossible — and to retreat and be on the safe side would look like supreme cowardice. So Jeffrey remained on the saddle and Whittaker pointed to the actuating lever.

'On your way, Mr. Collins. I shall remain until you come back, no matter how long.'

Jeffrey pulled over the actuating lever and immediately the strange power self-generated in the machine began to operate. There was a ghastly reeling sensation and Jeffrey gasped.

Everything — the laboratory, the night sky, the very surface of the earth, had vanished. He was in an impenetrable grey opacity through which, at times, light seemed to filter. Then it slowly became stronger.

Jeffrey looked about him, having the feeling that he was trying to peer through ground glass at something that would not quite take form. He strained his eyes to the uttermost but all he beheld was a blurred swiftly changing outline — murky, unresolved. Since he was not a scientist he could not realize that Time was hurtling past him so rapidly there was no fixed instant wherein anything could become tangible. There was only a vast and irresistible hurry, with the contours of future centuries building up and dissolving with the gossamer unreality of a dream . . .

But at last even this head-whirling enigma began to draw to an end as the mechanism on the incredible machine reached the limit of efficiency. With startling abruptness the cascading mysteries of intervening Time seemed to snap into place and Jeffrey was left panting for breath, still on the saddle of the machine, his taut fingers gripping the main stay-rod in front of him.

2

Vision of the future

Jeffrey looked about him and could scarcely believe what he saw. He was apparently on a rising stretch of ground outside a city. And what a city! It climbed in cathedrals of blue metal to a cloudless sky lighted by the brilliant sun. He stepped down to soft grass and took a breath of warm yet curiously invigorating air.

Five thousand years, Dr. Whittaker had said. Presumably, then, this was the world of 7012 A.D. . . . Jeffrey wanted to explore that city, but to do so would involve leaving the time machine, and if it should operate on its reverse mechanism when he was not there? On the other hand. Whittaker had said that some weeks might elapse here whilst only an hour of normal Time passed in 2012. And after all, there was a reason for having made

43

this amazing journey — to discover if Whittaker were still alive.

So Jeffrey began walking towards the city — down a long slope of smooth grass, which almost imperceptibly shaded off into blue metal roadway as the outskirts of the metropolis were reached.

Now, for the first time, Jeffrey saw the canyons of streets with metal bridges spanning them. Upon these bridges traffic moved in unending lines. Higher still were people going back and forth. This metropolis of 7012 was a gigantic termitarium of industry, and wherever he looked Jeffrey could see no end to its extent. He slowed to a halt, feeling dwarfed and incapable of understanding, much as a Neanderthal man might feel if he came suddenly upon a metropolis in 2012.

After several minutes Jeffrey glanced back to where the time machine stood on the rise of ground, then again he went forward, impelled by the fascination of it all.

Before long he came to the end of the roadway where it expanded into one of the central ground-level streets. Here there were men and women on the move, but no sign of traffic. Uncertain as to what would happen to him Jeffrey kept on going and so came into the midst of the passers-by. To his relief they paid him scant attention, probably accepting him as one of the community. The reason was not puzzling, for in clothing the men and women were little different to 2012, except perhaps for a greater richness of texture. In any event, Jeffrey's tweed suit was not so outlandish as to make him a figure of curiosity.

Gaining more courage, he moved with less furtiveness, studying the mammoth buildings as he went, and it gradually dawned in him that things were not so vastly changed after all. The names on some of the edifices were still recognizable as the English language, except for phonetic spelling.

Presumably, then, language would not be so much different — so when he came to an angle of the street where the human traffic was less dense Jeffrey took a chance and addressed a passing man. He looked very much like a 2012 lawyer, carrying a briefcase made of some curious metallic substance.

'Excuse me . . . ' Jeffrey got the words out and waited. To his relief he was answered in a perfectly normal tongue. He seemed genial, and disposed to help.

'Certainly. Can I help?'

'I don't want to take up your time, but what is this city? I'm a stranger here.'

'I judged that from your suit!' The passerby surveyed Jeffrey's attire and gave a faintly puzzled smile. 'From the provinces, I suppose? This is London, my friend.'

Jeffrey wrestled mentally. The time machine had not moved in space at all and had started on its time journey north of Birmingham it could only mean that in the interval London had spread up to the Midlands.

'London? Thanks. Don't think me too ridiculous, but what year is this?'

The man hesitated. 'You look tired. How about something to eat?'

'Well, I don't want to be a nuisance — '

'Not a bit of it. I'm in no hurry.'

Accordingly they went to an automat where, by radio control, a meal was supplied as he and his friendly guide sat at a quiet corner table.

'Now,' the citizen of 7012 said deliberately, as Jeffrey began to eat, 'what's this all about? I'm probably more curious than most because I'm one of the historians belonging to the Central Pool of Information. You are wearing clothes, which, to my experienced eye, suggests a period five thousand years old. Where on earth did you get them?'

'I've come out of Time,' Jeffrey replied frankly. 'Believe it or not, as you wish, but the machine which did it is not very far from here. I am on a tour of exploration to see what kind of a world it is five thousand years ahead of twenty twelve. Now laugh all you like.'

'I'm not laughing. This is another age of miracles, my friend, when only an idiot laughs at that which he doesn't understand.'

'Thanks.' Jeffrey gave a smile. 'May I ask more questions?'

'Surely. In turn you can answer some of

mine and confirm puzzling historical points. My name, incidentally, is Arlin Jag.'

'I'm Jeffrey Collins. Tell me, Mr. Jag, is there a familiar figure at present dominating the world called Irwin Whittaker?'

Arlin Jag shook his head firmly. 'No such person as Irwin Whittaker — though there is most certainly a world ruler.' He hesitated and glanced about him, then lowered his voice. 'I'm risking death by saying that the Mind is the most ruthless person I have ever known. Efficient and brilliant, yes, as well he ought to be with five thousand years of knowledge behind him, but definitely cruel. I don't give much for the chances of Mira Sandos who goes before him today on a charge of treachery.'

Jeffrey frowned. 'Mira Sandos? Who is that?'

'The most beautiful woman I have ever seen. The Mind will destroy her after torture, as he always does. Everybody loathes the Mind, but all obey him because they must. He rules the world and knows everything. Five thousand years have seen to that.'

'Five thousand years,' Jeffrey mused. 'In that case it must be Irwin Whittaker, but his name has dropped out. Where can I see him?'

For some reason an extraordinary expression had come to Arlin Jag's face. It was one of uncertainty and apprehension. Abruptly he got to his feet and put some queer currency down on the table.

'I must go,' he said briefly, taking up his case. 'That money will cover the meal. Put it in the receiver box by the door. Goodbye.'

'But, Mr. Jag — ' Jeffrey jumped up, but it was no use. Arlin Jag was on the move, and he kept going, finally vanishing in the street. Puzzled, Jeffrey stared after him, then feeling self-conscious in his 'ancient' clothes with the stares of men and women fixed upon him he too began to move. For some reason people got out of his way almost with deference as he headed for the doors. The money he put in the receiving box, which automatically opened the door for him — and so he stepped out into the street.

To him it seemed perfectly evident that Whittaker had survived the age-destroying drug and become master of the world. But how to make sure? Well, there might be a way to do that.

As he began walking, he again became aware of people glancing at him, and some of them appeared to shy away from him in fear. Finally he arrived at the conclusion it could only be his 'old-fashioned' clothes that were responsible.

At length he singled out an amiable-looking passer-by.

'Pardon me, but where can I attend the trial of Mira Sandos, who is to go before the Mind, today?'

The man looked astonished. 'With all the telecasts blazing it and every newscan full of it, you don't know that? The Temple of Justice — there, across the street.'

'Thanks.' Jeffrey crossed the street and entered the majestic edifice, ignoring the curious, puzzled glances cast at him.

So dense was the audience he could get nowhere near the front, so he took a position at the back, half concealed by an alcove. From here he could see the solitary stand in the centre of the vast floor whereon the prisoner would answer the charges; but the high seat of the judge — the Mind, ruler of the world — was hidden from him. Though he would not be able to see if the Mind were Irwin Whittaker he knew he would recognize the voice. In any case it had to be Whittaker. Had he not lived five thousand years?

Then came a solemn hush and the banging of a gavel. Jeffrey strained his neck but could not see the Mind. He did however see the prisoner as she was led out by two massive guards, slender chains fastened to her wrists.

Jeffrey realized he was looking upon the most lovely woman he had ever seen. She epitomized everything he expected in a woman. She transcended Betty as the sky transcends earth. Despite the distance between them he made out her graceful figure, lightly clad in curious draperies, the copper of her hair and the perfection of her features. She looked no more than twenty-five. Her stance when she came to

51

a halt was one of queenly defiance. In a matter of seconds Jeffrey fell in love and forgot he was five thousand years ahead of his own Time.

'Mira Sandos, you stand accused before your ruler and his dignitaries of high treason. What have you to say?'

Jeffrey tried to recognize the voice, but he could not. Possibly it might be that of Whittaker, changed by the centuries, but even then it sounded unfamiliar. Yet if it was not Irwin Whittaker, who else could have survived so long? Unless the drug had been marketed, and perhaps some other person ... Jeffrey lost himself in depthless speculation.

He heard the clear, sweet voice of Mira Sandos answering the charge against her, and that was as far as he got. Two guards had unexpectedly come up behind him and were motioning towards the doorway. Jeffery had no alternative but to go. Out in the corridor the reason was made clear to him.

'You have no pass,' the Chief Guard told him. 'Produce that and you may enter. Otherwise you have no right to be here.'

'I have no pass to offer,' Jeffrey answered, shrugging. 'Tell me, what do you think will happen to Mira Sandos?'

The guard studied him intently and Jeffrey saw in his eyes the same look that had been in the eyes of Arlin Jag before he had hastily excused himself. There had to be a reason for it, of course, but what?

Abruptly the guard turned away, motioning to his colleague, and Jeffrey was left alone.

Puzzled, Jeffrey stood thinking for a moment — then he made his way into the street and again became the focus of interested but respectful attention from the passers-by, and those still waiting to get into the Temple of Justice.

He started to walk slowly, disregarding the attention given to him, his mind centred chiefly on the lovely girl he had seen before the invisible figure of the Mind. Irwin Whittaker? Possibly. Possibly not. There might be a way of finding out if there were records anywhere . . .

Having become accustomed by now to

asking questions, Jeffrey asked a few more and towards mid-afternoon, beginning to feel hungry again, he found himself in the great Hall of Records wherein were kept the historical archives. The uniformed attendant gave him an odd look.

'Identification permit, please.'

'Is it compulsory?' Jeffrey asked impatiently.

'Certainly. You ought to know that everybody has to . . . ' the official broke off, and to his face came that peculiar expression that had appeared on the visages of Arlin Jag and the guards at the Temple of Justice.

'I merely wish to study the records. I don't need to identify myself for that, surely?'

'I'm afraid you do. Regulations demand it.'

So Jeffrey left again, his mission unfulfilled. It infuriated him in one sense, but in another he reflected that perhaps it was just as well. Back of his mind was the constant fear that if he delayed too long the time machine might start back without him, stranding him in this perplexing era — unless Whittaker could somehow contrive to send the machine back again to rescue him.

He made his way back through the gigantic city towards the road along which he had made his arrival, and to the rising stretch of ground where, to his infinite relief, the time machine was still standing. He got into the saddle and looked back towards the mighty city. He thought again of Mira Sandos and the strange drift of circumstances that had led him to see her. He knew he would never be able to forget her . . . Never.

Disconnecting the automatic mechanism he set the controls of the machine into reverse and moved the pointer to the 2012 mark. Then he closed the starting switch and instantly went reeling into the terrifying grey gulf.

Since he assumed the machine had not moved in space since his departure from Whittaker's laboratory, he also assumed he must return to the same spot — and his judgment was correct. Out of the murk there presently appeared the laboratory's familiar outlines, and then the big clock pointing to 7.45. Otherwise nothing was changed. The machine ceased functioning and he sat breathless and shaken, aware that he had been absent just ten minutes of normal time.

Dr. Whittaker was not in the laboratory, but the lights were still on. Possibly he had slipped into the house for a moment.

'Doc!' Jeffrey called eagerly, striding towards the connecting door. 'Doc, I've come back! I've seen — '

Jeffrey stopped, his attention frozen to a hand lying motionless just behind the leg of the main bench. It was the bench upon which there stood the various phials and reagents with which Whittaker had been mixing his age-destroying potion.

Jeffrey moved forward until he had a full view of Whittaker sprawled on the floor. The fixed, frozen look on his face made it unnecessary to take his pulse. He was dead.

Very slowly Jeffrey got to his feet again, too shocked to know what to do for the moment. His eyes strayed over the bench where still stood the various ingredients for the age-destroying drug. There was also the empty glass from which Whittaker had taken his dose — and, further away, the formula from which he had worked. Jeffrey picked it up, pondered it, and then put it in his wallet.

Being a sensible man Jeffrey knew he had only one course, so he took it. He telephoned the local doctor and the police, and when he'd done it he realized with a shock that he had put himself into an extremely difficult position. He certainly would not be able to explain about Time travel. And if he did if was doubtful if anybody would believe him.

The local sergeant came presently and took the particulars. The body of Dr. Whittaker was removed, then, cautioned that he must stay in the district, Jeffrey was allowed to go. It was 9,30 when he entered his own home.

'Well, it's about time!' Betty exclaimed. 'Where on earth have you been until this time? You said you were only going to make a few local calls.'

'Which is exactly what I did do. I called on Whittaker, though, on the way home.

And . . . and many things happened.'

Irritated by his late arrival Betty flounced out of the room and presently returned with the meal she had been keeping hot in the kitchen.

'If the electric bill's gone up, don't blame me,' she snapped. 'I had to use up current keeping this confounded meat warm for you.'

'Thanks, Bet,' Jeffrey said. 'Sorry if I put you out by not coming earlier — but as I said, things happened.'

'What things?' Betty's mood changed suddenly. 'Or do you mean something to do with that stuff for killing old age? The stuff we're going to make a fortune out of?'

'That's no longer a certainty,' he said. 'And Dr. Whittaker is dead, Bet.'

Betty stared. 'Dead? Dead! But — but what happened?'

Jeffrey rubbed a hand wearily across his forehead, and gave the details briefly. 'Either he died from natural causes, or there is the more horrible possibility that the drug he took killed him. If that should be true I'm going to have the devil of a job explaining myself.'

'But — but why should you? You didn't kill him, did you?'

Jeffrey gave a look and then compressed his lips. He motioned to the teapot and, mechanically, Betty drew forward the cups and saucers. After she poured the tea, Jeffrey explained exactly what had happened and it left Betty with her mouth sagging.

'And do you actually mean to tell me that you travelled five thousand years into the future?'

'I did.'

'But it's ridiculous! It's — '

'I tell you I did!' Jeffrey roared. 'Stop bleating!'

Betty blinked in amazement.

'Sorry,' Jeffrey muttered. 'My nerves are shot to bits after what I've been through.'

His mind was clouded with a multitude of worries, predominant among which was the death of Irwin Whittaker. More dimly still he remembered a lovely young woman who would not be born yet more for nearly five thousand years. Mira

Sandos . . . How different from Betty! How different indeed that whole city had been. Efficient, massive. The product of careful organization.

He ate his meal because he knew he must, then when it was over he took the formula of the age-destroying drug from his pocket and studied it.

'What's that?' Betty asked curiously, pausing in the act of clearing the tea things.

'Never mind.'

Feeling he could not tolerate her any longer Jeffrey got up and strode from the room slamming the door behind him. This formula, handled in the proper way, was worth a fortune — certainly not the thing for his talkative and empty-headed wife to gabble about to her friends. Jeffrey made up his mind that later he would study the formula privately. For the time being it would be best to hide it.

Going to the bedroom he put the formula in an old steel cashbox, which rarely contained any savings. Locking it, he tossed it through the window into the back garden. Coming downstairs again he found Betty in the kitchen washing up the dishes.

'Finished running about?' she asked. 'Usually you help.'

'I'm busy.' Jeffrey grunted, and went out into the garden.

He was absent about ten minutes. In that time, with the shovel from the woodshed, he had buried the steel box near the solitary apple tree. He came back into the kitchen with dirty hands and a preoccupied expression.

'Been gardening?' Betty asked sourly.

'Oh leave me alone, can't you? I've got a lot on my mind!'

With a sniff Betty swept from the kitchen. Jeffrey scowled, washed his hands and then followed her — to locate her coiled up on the chesterfield before the fire, a novel in her hands.

Settling in the chair opposite Jeffrey surveyed her without being conscious of it. There had been a time when he'd admired her rounded figure and dimpled chin. That was before he'd discovered how lazy she was — and before he had seen Mira Sandos . . . He could still see her in his mind's eye, the chains at her wrists, her superb figure as she had stood before the invisible figure of the Mind —

'It couldn't have been Whittaker!' he found himself saying unexpectedly, and Betty lowered her book to look at him.

'Now what are you talking about?'

'Whittaker. I wondered whether it was he or not five thousand years hence. It couldn't have been since he died tonight. Point is — who is it? Who will it be?'

'How should I know? If you'd behave like an ordinary husband instead of getting tangled up with mad scientists maybe we'd be happier.'

Jeffrey got to his feet. 'I'm going to bed, Bet. I feel pretty much off-colour after all I've been through . . . '

All he received was a shrug, so he left the room and hurried upstairs.

Jeffrey lived in constant fear of how much he was going to be involved in Whittaker's death. Three days later, he arrived home in the evening to find a police car in the street outside the house, and in the living room a chief inspector, a sergeant, and a startled-looking Betty.

'Evening, sir,' the heavier of the two men greeted as Jeffrey came in, and he rose from an armchair. 'You'll be Mr. Jeffrey Collins?'

'Yes, I'm he.'

'I'm a police officer, Mr. Collins.' The chief inspector held out his warrant card. 'I'd like a few words with you privately.'

'My wife knows as much as I do. There's no reason why you can't talk in front of her.'

'Sorry, sir. This is personal.'

Betty left the room slowly and closed the door, Jeffrey motioned to the armchair and the chief inspector seated himself again. Jeffrey crossed to the mantlepiece and leaned against it

'I suppose it's about Dr. Whittaker?' he asked

'It is, sir. We have the post-mortem report on his death and there are quite a few details that are obscure. I believe you were a friend of his?'

'An acquaintance would describe it better.'

'And a partner, Mr. Collins. His personal effects have revealed that much.

A partner in some mysterious kind of business connected with science.'

Jeffrey shrugged. 'Whittaker was a scientist and an inventor. I went into partnership with him because I believed that between us we could market quite valuable products.'

'Just so. Including a peculiar type of potion?'

Jeffrey was silent. The chief inspector got to his feet.

'Mr. Collins, I am not going to question you further because in doing so I'd step outside the letter of the law. What I am doing is charging you with the murder of Irwin Whittaker, and I have to warn you that anything you may say will be taken down in writing and may be used as evidence at your trial.'

Still Jeffrey did not say anything. He had been expecting all this.

'You will be formally charged at headquarters,' the inspector added. 'I must ask you to come along, sir.'

Jeffrey stirred. 'Before we go, might I ask what I am supposed to have done to Dr. Whittaker?'

'The medical report says poison. In the analysis there is a predominance of potassium sulphacyanide, a deadly poison. There are other elements mentioned, all of which tally with the dregs in the glass on the laboratory bench. As to the motive — you were apparently not on very good terms with Dr. Whittaker.'

'I was on the best of terms with him.'

'Not according to your wife, sir. You quarrelled with him before you became partners.'

'True, but it was nothing serious. In any case a wife can't testify against her husband.'

'I am aware of it. Mr. Collins. Nor will she, Mr. Collins. You have admitted you weren't on good terms with Whittaker at one point in your association. That's all I wished to verify.'

Jeffrey compressed his lips. 'I suppose I can tell my wife what has happened?'

'Certainly.'

★ ★ ★

And three weeks later Jeffrey's trial began — a trial conspicuous for many unusual features. He did not have an eminent lawyer to defend him. In fact he doubted if the most eminent legal man alive could defend him in such a complex dilemma. He was almost resigned to the belief that he was doomed. And with good reason when he heard the accumulation of evidence against him.

Where had he been during the period when Whittaker had died? To this there was no alibi — except the preposterous story that he had been five thousand years in the future! Had he, before the partnership, quarrelled with Dr. Whittaker? Yes. They both stood to make a fortune from some kind of formula? Yes. Jeffrey was forced into a corner by the very nature of the questions and felt himself going further under each time.

When had he administered the poison? He had no reply. His fingerprints were not on the glass which had been on the bench, but they could easily have been removed and Whittaker's hand clasped around the glass instead . . . The fact that he could not prove where he had been at the time of Whittaker's death was the most damning factor.

What was the strange product which, placed on the market, was going to make a fortune? Here again Jeffrey was silent — for two reasons. Since he could not make use of the formula, and because his death seemed inevitable now, he was determined nobody else should get it, analyze it, and discover why Whittaker had died instead of prolonging his life. He also felt convinced that a jury would not accept the idea that a potion for indefinitely prolonging life even existed. So again it was silence weakening his case.

And the queer machine in the laboratory? What was it? Silence. How was it possible to explain that it was a machine to travel Time? Not even scientists themselves would be able to help because none had been told of Whittaker's amazing journey, or Jeffrey's either. They might, of course, find out the machine's possibilities by tinkering with it, but embittered as he was Jeffrey saw no reason to enlighten anybody. It did not occur to him in his confusion that to have explained the facts, fantastic though they were, might have been the means of proving his innocence.

He gathered that the time machine was in the hands of the police at the moment, together with the late Whittaker's effects. Not that it mattered . . .

When he was brought back into court after the jury had considered its verdict he learned that there were several points not entirely proven by the prosecution. He was not guilty of murder, but manslaughter. He accepted the edict in silence and heard the judge pronounce a sentence of fifteen years . . .

Jeffrey compressed his lips. He caught a glimpse of Betty in the crowded court-room, and then he was led away — and it was a week later before his thoughts came back into focus amid the grey, impregnable walls of the penitentiary.

Fifteen years! And with what deadly slowness they passed. 2013 — 2014 — 2015. At first Betty visited the prison regularly; then gradually she became less attentive and finally stopped coming altogether. Jeffrey did not know what had become of her. He was left to himself and with only one thought that pleased him.

He could still dwell on the vision of Mira Sandos, and it was this that made him increasingly determined to find the time machine when he was released from jail. Unless scientists had discovered its powers he was the only man on earth who knew how to operate it. And he meant to depart from this Age completely, to go ahead again in a few years in precedence to Mira Sandos and learn all about her before the grim incident that had brought her before the all-powerful Mind.

From newspapers and broadcasts allowed into the prison he discovered that the queer contraption invented — so it was supposed — by Whittaker, was now in the British Museum as a curio, no scientist having been able to find out what it was supposed to be. So perhaps for that reason, it was relegated to the department for archaic and 'peculiar' discoveries. Apparently no scientist had investigated the matter.

This was probably because Whittaker had always been contemptuous of other scientists because they had failed to acknowledge his underlying greatness.

Jeffrey was resolved that upon release from prison he would somehow break into the Museum and, after that —

But in making this resolve Jeffrey reckoned without the tide of affairs in the world. The third World War exploded in 2018.

To Jeffrey and the inmates of the prison, it was a cauldron that bubbled and surged around them without actually affecting them. Times without number they were compelled to seek shelter far below the penitentiary, and night and day they heard the scream of jet planes and missiles and the thud of bombs, merging with the months into the mightier concussion of atom bombs.

Their livid, unholy light blazed through the prison and inflicted ghastly burns on those inmates who happened to be directly in line with the blast. Perhaps because he was not really interested in whether he lived or died Jeffrey escaped unhurt.

Prison regulations were relaxed a good deal so that constant radio and television news could be received by the prisoners — and the more they heard the more they realized that there seemed to be no ordered generalship on either side any more.

Nearly every city was in ruins; there were millions of maimed and homeless, but Earth as a planet still existed when the war abruptly ended. The peoples themselves of both sides, sickened of bloodshed and ruin, had turned on their leaders and called a halt.

In 2019, Jeffrey was assigned to a labour group clearing up war ruins. There was a small bare subsistence wage and a hell of a lot of work — but at least he was in London, or the twisted remains of it, and the last thought in his mind was to help rebuild this wilderness of twisted steel and blasted masonry. He had in mind the vision of a city where it climbed to the cobalt sky — of grace, and balance, and achievement, and a lovely girl named Mira Sandos.

His one aim was to find the British Museum quickly. This, though, proved more difficult than he had expected for the guards of the labour gang were exceptionally vigilant, with orders to shoot any breakaway worker on sight.

Exactly who was ruling the country Jeffrey had no idea. It was clearly not military law, and apparently neither side had won a decisive victory — so evidently civilization had degenerated into a few 'stronger than the rest' men taking control in their respective countries in an effort to restore order out of chaos.

Now and again Jeffrey wondered about Betty — not with any affectionate feelings, since she had evidently abandoned him; but he did remember that she had been his wife and there had been a time when he had genuinely loved her. He had to know what her fate had been . . .

He was no longer a quiet-spoken traveller but a grim-faced man nearing middle age, the lines hard around his mouth. Good-looking, yes, he had always been that, but with the stamp of immeasurable bitterness upon him. Life, so far, had been a pretty grim business and shot through with rank injustice.

Then, at long last, came his chance to make a dash for the British Museum. The labour gang he was with moved to the rubble of Bloomsbury. And the museum was still there!

Jeffrey slid from the truck as it wheeled round a corner and hid himself amongst the ruins. He waited until it was dark and then headed down Great Russell Street. But only the walls of the museum were standing — the interior was utterly destroyed. He could have cried with anger and disappointment. The whole museum was an illusion — a shell that looked normal from a distance. The shell of a massive building with the interior lost forever. Gone with the destruction was a machine that could travel from this mad, desperate Age into an assured and majestic future.

All night afterwards he wandered about the ruined city, too disconsolate to care much what happened to him. It was not far from dawn when he came to Hampstead, on a higher level than the shattered metropolis. He sank down on a high mound of ground, oblivious to the cold wind blowing through his thin working clothes, and surveyed the fires of the survivors winking in the night like fireflies. Human beings, intent on building up their lives again through many weary years. At that moment, as he thought of the grim vista ahead of him, Jeffrey came to contemplating suicide as any man can . . .

He was deeply depressed. Then he remembered something. Somewhere to the north of Birmingham there was a steel box buried under an apple tree. In the intervening years, so intent had he been on considering the possibilities of the time machine, he had forgotten about the formula he had hidden. If it could be recovered he could study it and perhaps find out what was wrong with it to bring about the death of Irwin Whittaker. He might, if he could rectify the error, market the product even yet and secure for himself some financial stability.

There were trains running and he had just enough money from his wages to pay a one-way fare to the Midlands. That he looked a hard-faced, half-bearded man in the dirty clothes of a worker did not signify.

He expected to be arrested, but was not. It meant that having made good his escape from the labour force he had been written off. In any case the authorities had far more to bother about than try to find one man; so Jeffrey found himself more or less undisturbed.

Birmingham proved to be in better shape than London. The region where he had once lived was almost untouched by bombs. Even his home was still there, dilapidated and needing paint. He opened the gate, strode up the short walk, and rapped on the door. A window opened in the weak morning sunlight and a round face with grey untidy hair wisping about it peered out.

'Betty!' Jeffrey gasped, staring up at her.

The silence was intense for a moment as Betty went through the effort of recognition — then when the truth dawned upon her she slammed down the window. Jeffrey half expected she would hurriedly come to open the door, but nothing happened.

Raising his elbow he smashed the glass, then reached inside and unfastened the catch. Swinging the door wide he strode across the small hall and up the stairs. At the landing he stopped, taking in the scene.

Betty was just outside the main bedroom door, a frayed dressing gown dragged about her floppy figure. She had become old-looking and fat in the intervening years. Not that Jeffrey paid much attention to her: his eyes were fixed on a man of uncertain age in a soldier's trousers and shirt. He was a little in front of Betty and seemed to be preparing for trouble.

'How — how did you get here?' Betty whispered.

Jeffrey did not answer. He gave a long, bleak stare and then hurried down the stairs. Going into the kitchen he hunted for food, packing his pockets with what meagre provisions he could find. This done he went into the weed-tangled garden and began digging under the apple tree. He knew that every move was being watched. Though he did not take the trouble to glance up over his shoulder he could feel two pairs of eyes fixed on him from an upstairs window.

He dug up the steel box. It was somewhat rusted but the corrosion had not bitten right through. A blow of the spade snapped the hasp and Jeffrey yanked the lid back quickly. The formula was still there, just as he had left it. Musty, but undamaged.

Throwing the shovel to one side he put the formula in his pocket, then without so much as a backward glance left the garden by the back gate and kept on walking.

By noon, Jeffrey had convinced himself that Betty no longer existed. For all practical purposes she was dead and he was a single man again — and in his pocket was a formula which might give him financial eminence in the years to come — the hard, gruelling years while Man patched up the ruins he had brought down for himself.

And for Jeffrey it was the start of a hard road, too. He did not stop to investigate the formula: there were more immediate matters to settle. He had to have money to keep him alive, some kind of a job with enough leisure to permit him to study. Things being what they were there was no difficulty in finding employment and the fact that he admitted he was a deserter from a prison gang made no difference. Harassed authorities were no longer concerned with a man's depredations — only the fact that he was strong and willing to work.

3

Betty returns

Towards the end of April 2020 he had used his natural intelligence and industry to promote himself from the job of builders labourer to that of construction foreman. Few liked him. He was hard-mouthed and ruthless. The life he had led and the beating he had taken had about destroyed whatever sentiment he had once possessed. He had a home of sorts that he had built for himself and here, when at last he could relax a little, he spent his time brooding over the formula which Whittaker had copied in Atlantis thousands of years before.

Several times he thought of seeking the aid of some scientist who might better interpret the formula; then each time he set his face against it. He even preferred to remain in ignorance of the formula's real power rather than bring in a second person who might cheat or even kill him. Thus deep was the measure of his suspicion of the human race in general.

So he went on working and experimenting. He bought some white mice and tried the formula in different strengths on each one of them. They all died at different times during 2023; so in 2024 he bought another batch and tried again tirelessly, working when he could in the little room at the back of his home.

In his ordinary work he was progressing. From construction boss he was promoted to a directorship in the British Rehabilitation Company, and at the end of 2024 he was managing director, his hair turning grey and his face inflexible. He now had under his control practically all the reconstruction of Britain — a position that elevated him to national importance.

He began to discover the few men who were trying to restore order to the shattered country. It was not a government in the accepted sense — rather a group of six men who, by their cornering of indispensable raw materials, had the country in their pockets.

Jeffrey still had his white mice to attend to — and one mouse in particular. It had been given the latest variation of the formula in January 2024, and now it was August, with the white mouse still scampering merrily around its cage. The time had come to make the final test. If the drug had worked at last, then by this time the mouse must have built up an anabolistic reaction to all substances likely to destroy it. Especially poisons. Suppose, then — ?

So Jeffrey gave the white mouse pure cyanide of potassium and then spent a whole evening watching for the result. With increasing amazement he found that the white mouse was quite unaffected. In fact, it ate a meal an hour after taking the poison and seemed to be none the worse. Perhaps there might be a sudden reaction later?

There was none. For a week Jeffrey kept watch over it, and by this time was fully decided that he had at last found the correct application of the formula. Irvin Whittaker had been too confident and too hurried, had not tested the stuff on another organism approaching the human in sensitivity. And, as too much of some drug can kill in one instance, and yet in an immeasurably slighter amount bring untold benefit, so there was a hairline also in the amounts needed to create the age-destroying drug . . .

And now? Jeffrey weighed the position very carefully, as men had ever been faced with such an incredible choice. On the one hand he was quite convinced that if he marketed his product he could net a tremendous fortune, but if he kept the secret to himself he could outlive every living person, become eternal through thousands of years, until —

The Mind? Could it be that circumstances were to make him the Mind? That shadowy, impersonal being whom he had never seen? Had it been more than just chance that he had not been able to glimpse the Mind during his visit to the future? Had there instead been some complex Time barrier that had made it mathematically impossible for him to see his own self?

But in spite of the tempest of argument raging within him he knew what he was going to do. Cheated of using the time machine to journey again into the future and meet Mira Sandos, there was this other way of doing it. Living through the thousands of years until he caught up with the period when she must appear.

This decision reached, he informed his secretary that he would be absent for the next day or so and, that evening, he mixed exactly the right quantity of potion and then stood for a moment with it in his hand.

He knew now how the unfortunate Irwin Whittaker must have felt when he had performed similar actions. Silent, alone in his small laboratory, Jeffrey surveyed the emerald-coloured liquid, hesitated as he looked at the still-happy white mouse that had taken poison — and then he drank. With a gesture of finality he flung the emptied glass down and watched it splinter on the floor.

He had destroyed old age. He could live on and on, in this ruin of a world. And since it was a ruin there was only one course for a man in his position — take control in the quickest way possible.

For two days he was ill as the potion found a balance in his system; then he became aware of remarkably increased strength and mental agility. The formula stolen from Atlantis was the elixir of the gods indeed.

In his capacity as head of British Rehabilitation he exerted his authority to the full — so much so that the men above him, netting fortunes from the materials they were supplying, began to object. Brookings of the Steel Combine was the first to say so openly.

'It's got to stop, Collins,' he said, one morning. 'You're taking too much on yourself.'

'Am I?' Jeffrey smiled coldly. 'As head of this firm I'm entitled to act as I please, and I shall continue to do so.'

'Not with our sanction!' Brookings snapped.

'No, without it,' Jeffrey said calmly.

Brookings got to his feet in sudden anger: 'Look here, Collins, what do you think you're doing? You can't override the government that I and my colleagues represent. You have given instructions for the most far-reaching building pro-grammes and never even consulted us. You can't do it!'

'But I have, and I shall not rescind a single order. It is not that which is worrying you, Brookings. It is the fact that this new building programme doesn't take you or your friends into account financially. I have found several smaller firms willing and able to turn out the steel and building materials we need without recourse to your massive combine. In the same way I have cut out your colleagues who usually supply timber, wiring, piping, stone, and so forth.'

'Which is rank betrayal!' Brookings shouted. 'We men at the top have got to work together.'

'I think differently, Brookings. You and your compatriots are a monopoly, and a monopoly should be broken.'

'But why? If we don't sell we're ruined.'

'I know.' Jeffrey sat back in his chair calmly. 'That's the general idea. If you cannot be productive you must perish.'

'But dammit, it's preposterous! Why should we perish when we're the backbone of the country?'

'I disagree. You are a bunch of self-righteous humbugs intent only on your own enrichment at the expense of the masses. I have decided I have no further use for you.'

Brookings stared. 'You, only a managing director, are daring to dictate to the government?'

'Don't waste my time with that nonsense, Brookings.' Jeffrey waved a hand impatiently. 'You do not constitute a government. You and your friends are self-elected and not the choice of the people. You just cashed in on the aftermath of war and had grand notions about soaking the war-survivors. We have before us a planet which has to be built anew, and I know how to model it on the right lines.'

'So now you're a visionary?' Brookings sneered.

'Perhaps.' Jeffrey looked at him absently. 'At least I know what this city can look like five thousand years from now.'

'You can't get away with this, Collins,' Brookings snapped. 'As long as you played the game our way we were willing to give you every chance — but now your head has swollen you need stripping of all authority. And you will be! Remember, you're an ex-jailbird.'

'I was falsely accused by a government which has been blasted out of existence. That affair is dead.'

'Some people have long memories. You haven't heard the last of this. As for that remark about having seen how London will look in five thousand years, I assume you were being facetious?'

'I was never more serious in my life.'

Which was too much for Brookings. He clenched his fists, then without saying any more he stormed out of the office and slammed the door. Jeffrey smiled faintly to himself and continued with his work.

In ten minutes Brookings had reached his own headquarters in the city centre with his five colleagues. In an hour they were in conference with him.

'The man's crazy!' Brookings insisted.

'Instead of working through us he fools about with piffling little firms who haven't a tenth of our productive capacity. It doesn't make sense.'

'I think it does,' said the Timber King morosely. 'I've always had a feeling that Jeffrey Collins would prove a rod in pickle for us one day — and now I'm sure of it. It's perfectly obvious that if he is in control of rebuilding Britain, as he is, and refuses to use our materials, we automatically take a terrific hiding. We can sell abroad, of course, bur Collins may stop that too, in time.'

'But he can't! He isn't the government! We are!'

The men glanced at each other and then the Timber King spoke for them.

'Purely an arbitrary term, Brookings. You've overlooked the fact that in this day and age power goes not to a self-elected body like us but to the man with the greatest monopoly of materials — and in his position as head of British rehabilitation Collins has that monopoly. We got him into that high chair and to save ourselves we must unseat him.'

'Kill him?' Brookings asked, and nobody spoke for a moment.

'Millions have died in the war,' one of the men said. 'I cannot see that one more can make much difference. But I think it must be done subtly because Collins definitely has a hold over the people.'

Brookings said: 'I had thought of exposing his prison sentence. We know all the particulars.'

'It would carry no weight these days,' the Timber King decided. 'There may be a better way. Tell me what you think of this . . . '

* * *

In consequence of what he had to say, that same evening Betty Collins found herself in the office of Brookings. She had not the vaguest idea what was going on. All she knew was that two men had called upon her and, politely but firmly, had insisted that she go with them. Believing them police officers and that she had been mistaken for somebody who had committed a criminal offence, she had obeyed. Now, in her shabby coat, her hat awry, she stood looking at the famous Brookings across his big desk.

'My apologies, Mrs. Collins, for such unorthodox methods,' he smiled, rising and settling a chair for her. 'Do be seated, please — All right,' he added to the two men, and they left the office.

Frowning, Betty waited, still trying to fathom why she had been brought to the headquarters of the most powerful man in the country.

'My agents located you quite promptly, Mrs. Collins,' Brookings continued, resuming his seat at the desk. 'I feel that you are the kind of woman who would be willing to render the country a service — for a consideration of course.'

'Far as I can see I've no choice,' Betty answered sullenly. 'You are supposed to be at the head of the government Mr. Brookings, so whatever you order I must do.'

'I am the nominal head of the government at the moment, yes, but I would prefer you to forget that. What I have to ask is more in the nature of

— well, a personal favour.'

'Oh? But what in the world could you want with me? I'm just one of the millions of women who survived the war. I have to work to keep myself alive since my husband deserted me.'

'You are still the wife of Jeffrey Collins, and in that capacity you can be useful to me and the country as a whole — if you reunite with your husband.'

Betty laughed shortly. 'Your intelligence department must be slipping, Mr. Brookings. Jeff is finished with me completely. He misunderstood the fact that a soldier was billeted in my home and — well, you can imagine how it looked when not explained.'

'I am not interested in personal details, Mrs. Collins. Your husband is becoming a menace to the peace and security of this country just when it is trying to get on its feet again. You must be aware of how much authority your husband is grasping.'

'Yes, I'm aware of it. Quite unusual for him, too. He never used to be the pushing sort even if he was a commercial.'

'He has control of certain raw materials,' Brookings continued. 'If any stranger tried to learn the names of these various small companies your husband would become suspicious. But you could no doubt find out the names without difficulty if you patched up your differences with him.'

'Possibly. But what good would a few names do you?'

'If I knew the firms he has set in competition against me I could destroy his hold over them. The point is: are you willing to help? You are the only one who can, and if you do not there will inevitably come a day when your husband will dominate the country and enforce his every wish upon it. More — he might dominate the world. That must be prevented at all costs.'

'I can't see why. I've read what Jeff intends to do for the people and it all sounds pretty reasonable to me.'

Brookings said patiently: 'You must allow me to decide what is right for the country — and I repeat that your husband is a menace. I even have doubts as to his sanity. Once, in conversation, he told me he knew exactly how London would look in five thousand years' time. Well, I ask you!'

'He said that? Oh, he was probably referring to the trip into the future he made just before he was arrested.'

'Trip into the future?' Brookings gave a start. 'What in the world do you mean?'

'I mean that Dr. Whittaker, the man Jeff was supposed to have killed — though I'm quite sure he did no such thing — found or invented a time machine. Jeff tried it, went five thousand years ahead, and then came back. I don't know what happened to the machine but I think Jeff has the design of it. He buried it in the back garden before he went to prison, and dug it up again when he came out. I didn't realize what he'd done until he did dig it up, otherwise I'd have had a look for myself.'

'You actually mean to tell me that your husband has the secret of travelling Time?' Brookings demanded, incredulous.

'I'm convinced he has.'

Brookings got to his feet and stood thinking. 'But what a difference this makes!' he muttered, half to himself. 'No wonder he is so assured if he knows what future time holds. What could I not do with a secret like that! Make my investments after studying their future development . . .'

He looked again at Betty. 'I am going to make a bargain with you, Mrs. Collins. A lot hinges on whether you still have any affection for your husband. If you have, you will never be able to accomplish your purpose, but on the other hand — '

'You can rest assured, Mr. Brookings, that I haven't a spark of affection left for Jeff. How could I after the way he walked out on me?'

'I am remembering that women are sometimes strange in their affections. They love even whilst pretending to hate. That, however, is a chance I must take. If you can obtain for me the secret of this time-travel, together with the names of the opposition firms I need, I will pay you fifty thousand pounds.'

'That's not much for the risk I'd have

to take, besides running contrary to my inclinations.'

Brookings looked surprised for a moment and then he grinned.

'I didn't suspect you were a business woman, Mrs. Collins.'

'I'm not, but I know I'm the only one who can help. I'll do it for a hundred thousand and not a penny less.'

'Very well.' Brookings compressed his lips.

'And before I make a single move I want everything in writing. I can't trust you any more than you can trust me.'

'That can be arranged immediately.'

'And finally,' Betty added, 'I wish to be dressed properly. I can hardly approach Jeff in clothes like these.'

Brookings eyed her and reached for the interphone . . .

★   ★   ★

Jeffrey, following a conference with his own immediate colleagues, in which he outlined his plans and his intention of overriding the clique that called itself a government, worked late in his office that evening, drafting new plans for the reconstruction of Britain and making the first advances to other countries in an effort to make them fall in with his ideas. He was a man who had no need to take heed of time. If the anabolistic reaction within worked out normally he had thousands of years in which to achieve his objective. The one thing that still puzzled him was whether he was to be the Mind of the future, or had another factor still to come into the situation? And with the time machine destroyed there was no way of discovering the answer except by surviving generation after generation.

Then towards eight o'clock the night porter showed Betty into the office. Jeffrey, though advised by the interphone of her coming, still could not quite believe it. He stood beside his desk, gazing at the smartly-dressed woman on the edge of middle age who now walked towards him. Beauticians had done a good job for her.

'You can't believe it, can you?' Betty asked.

Jeffrey motioned to a chair and contemplated her.

'Is this a social call?' he asked shortly.

'I'd prefer to call it a reunion between husband and wife.'

Jeffrey sat down. 'To be quite frank, I want nothing further to do with you. I can't understand why you've come looking for me.'

'Because you jumped to conclusions when you saw that soldier at home. He was billeted on me. That's all.'

Despite the years which had passed Betty still had claims to being fairly good-looking, unless the beauty experts had done an exceptionally good job.

'Well, why did you come here?' Jeffrey asked.

'I want you to believe, Jeff, that I still love you.' Betty said quietly.

'I find that hard to believe. You stopped coming to see me when I was in prison: you had a strange man in the house when I came upon you unexpectedly, and now you've realized I have achieved a certain eminence, I suppose, so have decided to cash in on it. Very well, I'll see you have a generous allowance. Let it go at that.'

Betty's eyes never left Jeffrey's face. 'You do hate me, Jeff, don't you?'

'Not hate you. Just disappointed in you. There was a time when — ' Jeffrey made a restless movement. 'Oh, why go into that now?'

'I stopped visiting you in prison because I was taken ill. I'd just got to my feet again when the war came, and I had to do my bit. I did it — driving an ambulance.'

Jeffrey looked astonished. 'You, of all people, drove an ambulance?'

'Why not? I was willing to do my bit. When the war was over I found work of a different kind, thanks to that soldier who was billeted with me. You got the wrong idea about him. He was an angel. That we had to live together was one of the exigencies of war. Jeff, that is the truth,'

Jeffrey got to his feet and moved slowly towards Betty's chair. She watched him, a far less flippant woman than she had been in her younger days.

'Life's too short to quarrel, Jeff,' she said. 'I came here tonight after a good deal of heart-searching. After all, I'm still your wife and knowing you I am sure you were never cut out to be a bachelor. Can't we — can't we patch things up?'

'I wish I could believe all this,' Jeffrey muttered; then his attitude suddenly changed. 'I suppose I was pretty boorish at times. Like the evening when I went out and buried the — when I buried something in the garden. I remember I nearly bit your head off.'

Betty smiled a little. 'I have been promised a hundred thousand pounds if I can wheedle out of you the secret you buried in the garden. Design of the time machine, wasn't it?'

'What did you say? Been offered a hundred thousand? I'll make one guess — Brookings!'

'Yes, Brookings. That's why I'm dressed in this finery. He paid for it. All so I could make an impression on you. But I have been rather clever, Jeff. I made him pay me fifty thousand down, the other half to follow when I get the information he wants. So you see, I'm not so slow, am I? On the one hand I'm proving my loyalty to you, and on the other I've cleaned up fifty thousand,'

'Is this absolutely true?' Jeffrey asked seriously. 'Did Brookings rope you in so you could betray me?'

'That was his idea, and he thinks I'm going to do it. But I never meant to. In spite of what you think there is no other man in my life except you. I want you back with all my heart. If I didn't really still love you do you think I'd have told you as much as I have?'

'No. No, I suppose you wouldn't.'

The one thing that had been clouding Jeffrey's relentless ascendancy so far had been the lack of a woman's affection. He was the kind of man who could not exist without it — and the vision of an ineffably lovely creature some five thousand years hence was, at best, a remote objective. He had to think of now, and legally he was still Betty's husband.

'I don't see what more I can say to prove my feelings,' Betty murmured.

'There's nothing more, Bet, and I'm satisfied. Let us say that misunderstanding forced us apart — that and war. Let's forgive and forget. In any case, I need you. You'll never be a brilliant woman, but at least you have balance. You can be the mainstay of the man who intends, in time, to rule the world.'

'Rule the world?' Betty repeated slowly. 'Yes, that's what Brookings said. And he means to stop you! He's afraid of you, Jeff, which is why he sent me — the person closest to you — to try and discover your secrets. He is particularly anxious to know the firms with which you're dealing.'

'Yes, I daresay he is.' Jeffrey gave a taut smile. 'And he also wants to know what I dug out of the garden, does he? Just how did he know about that?'

'I let the information slip unintentionally, and I'm afraid I made things worse by saying it was probably the design of the lost time machine.'

'Which Brookings wants?'

'More than anything else in the world. He said something about studying future investments and then cashing in on them.'

'Naturally he'd think of that,' Jeffrey

said. 'But he's going to be unlucky. I have no design of the time machine, and the machine itself has been destroyed. Or I assume so.'

Betty frowned. 'Then what did you bury in the back garden?'

For a long moment Jeffrey hesitated, then he came to a decision.

'You've been frank with me, Bet, so I'll be frank with you,' Jeffrey replied, after a long pause. 'It was the formula for neutralising old age.'

'That!' Betty looked disgusted. 'Some use it proved to be when it killed Whittaker.'

'It killed him, yes, but not me. You're looking on a man who has many thousands of years ahead of him.'

Betty was looking dazed, as she always did when faced with the improbable, especially a scientific issue.

'I hope to live five, or even seven thousand years,' Jeffrey continued. 'Not that I expect you to believe it. I don't even expect you to believe that I am virtually eternal. So I'll prove it.'

He turned to a small safe and from it

brought a bottle of deep purple colour labelled 'Cyanide of Potassium'. Before Betty could grasp his intentions he had poured some of the poison into the container from the water carafe and then swallowed it.

'Jeff, what have you done!' Betty jumped up and hurried over to him, clutching at his shoulders. There was genuine horror on her face.

'Your actions tell me a lot,' he said, tossing the cup away. 'You really do care what happens to me, so I'm satisfied we can start again.'

'You mean it isn't really poison in that bottle?'

'Certainly it is! Genuine cyanide, and it would kill any ordinary man immediately. But not me. Poisons have no effect upon me. I've built up a resistance. Possibly bullets and dagger wounds might pass me by, too. It's a matter of adaptability. This is Whittaker's elixir as it should have been before the poor devil killed himself.'

'Then ... ' Betty stopped, still half afraid.

'I cannot die,' Jeffrey said. 'I have made

myself virtually eternal because I wish to live long enough to see — ' He hesitated, not wanting to admit he was also anxious to meet Mira Sandos again. 'To see the world I intend building come to its full maturity, as it will in five thousand years.'

'Could I be made eternal, too?' Betty questioned, and this startled him. If Betty, too, lived through the thousands of years until the time when Mira Sandos must appear, what then?

'Possibly,' he answered evasively. 'But you should give it careful thought. You can't lightly accept the idea of almost eternal life. Think what it means — '

'I have. If you want me beside you I'll have to live as long as you, shan't I?'

Jeffrey turned. 'I'd better take you home. And it's in need of a woman's touch, too. It's a far better home than any we've had so far.'

So for the moment Betty said no more. Jeffrey led her from the office to the rear of the building where his car was standing. She sank into the soft upholstery and glanced about her at the fittings.

'You've come a long way, Jeff.'

'And I shall go a lot further.' He switched on the engine and the car glided out into the main street. 'I am one man distinct in all the world, Bet. Compared to every other human being I am eternal. It sort of does something to you when you get used to it.'

'You're not the Jeff I used to know. You're — different.'

'Maybe ambition's changed me,' he said, and dropped the subject. Betty did not bring it up again.

What neither she nor Jeffrey realized was that if you exact something from Nature she will claim repayment in some form or other. Always she must find a balance, and she was finding it in Jeffrey. In defeating normal law by prolonging his life indefinitely he had thrown himself out of focus with the scheme of things. Something was being exacted and its first signs were visible in his deep-rooted selfishness, the intensifying conviction that he was a god.

When Betty saw the home he had built for himself she was satisfied that she had made the right move in rejoining him. To her credit, she really meant to be loyal to him but she also meant to be sure that she would have all the things she longed for.

She prepared a meal much in the fashion of earlier days and she and Jeffrey ate mainly in silence. Then he said:

'The people are behind me and have come to accept me as the new ruler of their destiny, chiefly because I have devised so many programmes for their comfort; but as long as there is opposition my activities are limited. I must remove that opposition. Between me and the complete domination of this country there stand half a dozen men who deliberately engineered themselves into positions of authority in the hope of making fortunes. They're rotten right through, with Brookings the most rotten of all, Otherwise he would never have used you to try and get my secrets from me.'

'I suppose he thought any means legitimate,' Betty answered, musing.

'I shall kill him,' Jeffrey said, and Betty gave a start.

'Jeff, what on earth are you saying?'

'I am saying that Brookings must go, and after him the five other men who act as his satellites. No country can have two masters, and I have greater reason than anybody for being the master of this one.'

'Because you are eternal?'

'Isn't that reason enough?'

'But Jeff, what you are contemplating is murder! Whatever you may call it, it's still murder.'

'I prefer to call it elimination, in the same way as a general views a battle. He doesn't 'murder' the enemy: he destroys him.'

'But there's no comparison. Whatever else you may chose to call it, it's still murder!'

Jeffrey was silent, his face expressionless. Betty studied him, her brow wrinkled.

'How changed you are, Jeff. It couldn't be just prison that has made you like this, nor the injustice of the sentence you got. It's something else. You're inflexible — ruthless.'

'A man who is unique cannot afford to

be anything else.'

'And an egotist as well,' Betty finished, at which Jeffrey made an irritated movement.

'I'm not a commercial traveller any more in a cheap suburban house. I have a destiny and I shall fulfill it.'

'Maybe, but you don't expect me to condone murder, do you?'

'Elimination! And if you don't approve of what I intend to do, Bet, you know the remedy. I don't think you'll take it, either, you'd lose too much. Now forgive me, Bet, but I have things to do. We'll talk again later . . . '

Betty watched in moody silence as he left the room and, a few minutes later, drawing back the heavy drapes from the window, she saw the rear lights of his car vanishing down the driveway. For perhaps the first time in her life she realized that she had a tremendous responsibility. The days when she had taken Jeffrey for granted as a mild young man with a few argumentative tendencies had gone. She had reunited herself to a man who was evidently determined to smash down everything opposing him in an effort to fulfil what he regarded as his destiny. Perhaps he was mad — perhaps a lot of things. The fact remained that if she were to remain loyal she had a great deal to do.

4

The Scourge

Some fifteen minutes after this Jeffrey was driving through the battered city, his face set. He drew up outside one of the few great Mayfair residences that had survived the war. Hurrying up the steps he rang the bell and a tall manservant opened the door.

'Mr. Brookings in?' Jeffrey enquired briefly. 'I'm Jeffrey Collins.'

'Yes, sir. Won't you step inside? I'll let Mr. Brookings know.'

Jeffrey stepped into the big hall and waited. Then the man returned and with majestic movements led Jeffrey into the library. Brookings was in an armchair, cigar in his mouth, an alpaca jacket about his gross figure.

'Quite a surprise, Collins,' he said, getting up and extending his hand. 'Social call, or business?'

'Definitely business. What would I want wasting a social call on you?'

Brookings lowered his hand. 'All right, so you're peeved about something and want to have it out with me. I'm willing. Take a seat.'

'I can do this standing up,' Jeffrey retorted. 'I've an account to settle for you sending my wife to spy on me.'

Brookings did not betray his surprise. He waited, cigar in hand; then his gaze dropped to the automatic Jeffrey was holding.

'Stop being melodramatic,' Brookings advised. 'It won't get you anywhere. You've found out about your wife, so on that score I'm beaten. I'll try other ways.'

'Not with me you won't. I meant what I said.' Jeffrey raised the automatic. 'See this gun? Same type as they used in the war. Silent, and it never misses. Your dead body will be found with a bullet in it, but that doesn't concern me. All I need is time to get out of here, then I can handle the situation. With you and your colleagues out of the way I'll make the laws. So I can hardly be accused of murder.'

'Now look here, Collins, stop talking like an idiot and — '

There was a click from the automatic. Brookings' hand moved to the region of his heart and he tottered forward. Jeffrey caught him before he fell to the floor and manoeuvred him into the chair at the desk. His attitude looked as if he had fallen asleep.

Returning the automatic to his pocket Jeffrey turned to the French window, opened it, and stepped out in the night, closing the window behind him. In another thirty seconds he was driving away, quite heedless of the act he had performed. And there was more work to be done yet . . .

★ ★ ★

He returned to his home towards daybreak to find that Betty had fallen asleep in the lounge. As he entered she awakened suddenly and glanced towards the clock.

'Did you — ?' she began, and hesitated.

'Yes.' Jeffrey came over and stood

looking down upon her. With the sleep still in her face she looked faded — nothing like the Betty he had once known, and even less like a woman yet to be born . . . Mira Sandos.

'I have eliminated the opposition,' he stated. 'There was no other way for me to achieve complete domination. Starting from this moment I am the Dictator of Britain.'

'And you still wish me to stay beside you?'

'Isn't it you who wishes to stay beside me?'

'I am trying,' Betty said, 'to remember the Jeff I used to know, but with every hour you're changing. I still want to live with you, if only in the hope that I may be able to make you forget power.'

'You'll never do that, Bet.'

'I'll try. At least I'm human, which is more than you are.'

Jeffrey's eyes narrowed and he gripped her shoulders. 'What do you mean by that?'

'Ask yourself, after what you have been doing tonight. Would the old Jeff have done that?'

'I was a young man then. Now I'm mature. And you are a mature woman . . . Too much so, in fact.'

Anger flared in Betty's blue eyes. 'That's a rotten thing to say, Jeff! I'm thirty-six, four years younger than you.'

Jeffrey gave the icy smile of a man who knows his life is indefinitely prolonged.

'I want to remain at thirty-six for a very long time to come,' Betty added. 'I am your wife and I want to be made eternal — or nearly so — as you are.'

'So we're back to that again?' Jeffrey dropped his hands from her shoulders. 'You've considered what it means?'

'Yes. And I still want it.'

Jeffrey fell to thought. In five thousand years Mira Sandos would be in existence, and probably Betty would too. In five thousand years he would have grown mighty tired of her. In fact he was that already. She seemed useless, faded, inefficient. But a companion on the long road was desirable, even if it was only Betty.

'Very well,' he said abruptly. 'But remember: once you have taken the

114

potion there can be no turning back. There is no antidote as far as I know.'

'I don't want an antidote. All I do want is to be as you are, and see things the way you do. Then we can perhaps be more or less happy together. We certainly can't as we are because I can't fathom your attitude to everything. I have got to become hard, too. Destroy what bit of human sentiment I have left. You might as well. It never did me much good, anyhow.'

Jeffrey gave her a puzzled glance and then led the way from the room and to his laboratory at the back of the house. Despite the fact that he had been on the move all night he did not appear in need of sleep. His hands were steady, Betty noticed, as he poured out the potion into a phial and then handed it over.

'Drink it,' he instructed. 'It will make you feel like nothing on earth for a couple of days, then will come a vitality and sharpness of mentality such as you have never known. I wonder,' he mused, as he handed over the phial for the second time as Betty still hesitated, 'I wonder if the children of such as you and I would also be blessed with vastly long lives?'

'The children?' Betty studied the fluid critically.

'What is so remarkable about that? We never got around to it. It still isn't too late. Somebody must follow when the thousands of years have run out.'

Betty did not answer. She finished contemplating the potion and then drank it, making a grimace as she drained the glass.

'Tastes horrible,' she said.

'I know. Best thing you can do now is lie down until the first effects have passed off.'

She nodded and left the laboratory rather unsteadily. Jeffrey picked up the empty glass, inspected it, and then hurled it to the floor. He was not sure whether or not he had been a fool in giving way to Betty's wishes. She would remain with him now for the thousands of years, becoming more resistant to old age with every day that passed. In one year she would be invulnerable. It would not even be easy to eliminate her if she had grown tiresome . . .

The following day Betty was prostrate. Since it was no more than Jeffrey had expected he did what he could to make her comfortable, left instructions with the woman who daily ran the house for him, and then went about his usual affairs. He knew he appeared callous, and he had no wish to change it. It was becoming part of his make-up and he secretly revelled in it. With every hour the old Jeffrey Collins was disappearing and giving way before this new being with thousands of years to live.

The news of Brookings' death, and those of his five companions, had hit the headlines. In every case 'murder' was mentioned, but there did not seem to be anything anybody could do about it. Law had become extremely elastic and those officials who practised it were not at all sure of their ground. Things worked out exactly as Jeffrey had expected. Nobody acted, and he was left free. Possibly a good many suspected that he was the culprit, for the Brookings' butler must have talked — but to tackle the man who was rebuilding Britain and who had now automatically become a dictator was more than any law official cared to attempt.

So Jeffrey smiled and tightened his hold. He gathered his lieutenants around him, the men who were leaders in their own particular sections, and gave them fresh instructions.

The building programmes were enlarged. Everything that could be done for the people must be done. Here there was no callousness on Jeffrey's part. He meant to give the survivors of the war a square deal — but probably the ultimate purpose of his generosity was to see the mighty city of the future taking shape and to feel that he was its creator.

A week passed, time in which he had rarely been home, and in a quiet moment it occurred to him that by this time Betty ought surely to be well on the road to recovery.

But Betty was not improved. On the contrary she was critically ill. Jeffrey realized it the moment he arrived at her bedside for the first time in a strenuous week.

'Bet, what's the matter?' he asked anxiously, and there was a touch of the old Jeffrey in his voice.

'She's been like this, Mr. Collins, ever since you left me in charge of her,' said the housekeeper. 'Sort of fever she's got, I think.'

'Leave us alone, Mrs. Morgan, please. I'll attend to this.'

'Yes, sir.'

Jeffrey waited until the door had closed and then sat down on the edge of the bed, taking Betty's limp hand in his own.

She opened her eyes slightly in the glow of the table lamp and studied him.

'Just couldn't bear the thought of it, could you?' she whispered.

'Thought of what, Bet? I don't understand.'

'Yes you do. You poisoned me. The idea of my sticking at your side for thousands of years was too much, wasn't it? Now I know you don't really love me any more.'

'This is absurd!' Jeffrey protested, looking at her intently. 'I didn't poison

119

you, Bet. I need you more than anybody else in the world. Remember me saying about — children?'

'That isn't going to happen, Jeff. I'm dying, and you killed me.'

'For heavens' sake believe me!' Jeffrey entreated. 'I didn't poison you! I gave you exactly the same ingredients in that potion as I used on myself. I just don't understand this reaction.'

Betty was looking at him, through him into space, and her hand was very still. He glanced down at it and then back to her unwavering eyes. Finally he could stand it no longer. He leapt to his feet and half stumbled from the room, shouting for Mrs. Morgan. She came, wonder on her tired face.

'Take a look at my wife,' Jeffrey ordered, his voice brittle. 'It's more than I can do . . . '

He began to walk the corridor outside the bedroom as Mrs. Morgan vanished within it. In a moment or two she had returned, consternation on her face.

'Mr. Collins, she's — she's — '

'Dead,' Jeffrey said quietly. Then he

swung on her. 'Well, that's right, isn't it? Don't just stand there!'

'Yes, Mr. Collins, it's right. But I don't understand — '

'Neither do I. Get a doctor quickly. I'm going to the laboratory.'

Such an extraordinary decision at a moment like this was something else Mrs. Morgan could not understand, but she obeyed orders. His eyes hard, Jeffrey strode into his laboratory and slammed the door. Going to the bench he began to mix ingredients for the age-killing potion. When he had them to his satisfaction he looked at the white mice he always kept in a nearby cage for experimental purposes. Selecting one of the females he gave it a percentage of the potion and retained the remainder for later analysis.

He had just done it when he remembered something Irwin Whittaker had once said upon his return from Atlantis.

They had been words of vast importance though they had not seemed so at the time — 'All the time I was in Atlantis I never once saw a woman. Either there were none, or else they were kept in constant subjection. There is also another possibility: that all women in that Age were extinct for some reason, which would account for the later disappearance of the Atlanteans, there being no progeny . . . '

'Good God,' Jeffrey whispered, staring in front of him. 'No, not that! Not something fatal to the female but not the male! It couldn't be!'

Whirling around, he looked intently at the female mouse. At the moment it seemed none the worse. He hesitated and then hurried from the laboratory and back upstairs. Mrs. Morgan was just coming from the bedroom, closing the door. She looked white and shaken, far more than seemed natural under the circumstances.

'You did as I asked?' Jeffrey enquired.

'Yes, Mr. Collins. The doctor's coming right away . . . '

Jeffrey's eyes pinned her. 'Go on, say it! You believe I poisoned her!'

'No, no, I don't. It's just that Mrs. Collins kept on saying, over and over, that you did. So — so I — '

'There will be no inquest,' Jeffrey stated. 'My wife's death was . . . misadventure.'

There was fear in Mrs. Morgan's eyes. 'Yes, Mr. Collins. Just as you say. I'll go downstairs ready to admit the doctor.'

Jeffrey stood thinking, then his speculations were interrupted by a sudden thudding noise. He turned and looked at the head of the staircase — then he dashed forward just in time to see Mrs. Morgan finishing a helpless head-over-heels tumble from top to bottom.

So began the Scourge, its source in the home of the man who was determined to master the world.

It had begun with Betty Collins and had been transmitted to Mrs. Morgan, who had handled the body. The undertakers who handled both corpses inevitably came into contact with women in their own families and, unwittingly, transmitted death. In a week from the death of Betty Collins women were dying at an appalling rate and nobody knew how to combat the menace.

Jeffrey deserted his usual tasks in the city and worked with desperate energy in the laboratory. He was the only living person who could possibly discover what had caused the Scourge, because he was the only person who knew about the age-neutralising formula.

Haggard and weary he finally arrived at a possible solution, determined by a study of the potion itself and vivisection of the female white mouse which had died — its female companions following shortly afterwards. The answer was one which Jeffrey could not possibly keep to himself with every living soul in the country demanding an explanation and, if possible, a solution. Other countries, too, were in a fever of alarm lest their women, too, be relentlessly struck down.

All Jeffrey could do was broadcast his findings and at the same time try to make things as easy as possible for himself. Things were in the balance. The people might turn on him as the cause for everything.

'At the moment,' came his voice, from every loudspeaker in the city, 'there is no solution to the Scourge, unless the scientists can find one. I am not a scientist, but I can tell you what has happened. There is in existence a drug that can bring a life span to some seven thousand years to any male. It was the secret of the men of Atlantis and was handed down to me in a way I shall not disclose. I am, in effect, eternal. My wife asked, quite naturally, that she too might be made as long-lifed as myself, so I gave her exactly the same ingredients as I gave myself.

'It appears, however, from a study of a female white mouse, that the potion has a totally different effect on the female system to that of the male. There is not the same resistance and death ensues. What is more ghastly, a 'dew of death' is left behind — so often spoken of in the Bible in ancient times, you will remember — and this dew is highly contagious to any other female, and cannot be removed by washing. The merest contact with it, though perhaps only transmitted by the hands of a male which has been in contact with the dew, can produce fatal results. The female skin absorbs it; the male does not. That, in effect, is the cause of the Scourge. The morticians who handled the bodies of my wife and Mrs. Morgan, my housekeeper, passed it on to their womenfolk. They in turn passed it to others, and now it is everywhere, striking down the female in every species at a terrifying rate. I know of no way to stop it. Records suggest that the people of Atlantis, thousands of years ago, also suffered the Scourge and in consequence died because there were no more women. The only answer, perhaps, is — synthesis.'

As Jeffrey had expected, his statement infuriated the people. They came in droves to the city headquarters but he took good care to shield himself behind the militia. The only people permitted to see him were men in charge of the various social services he had devised. He found most of them desperate with anxiety.

'Mr. Collins, you don't seem to realize what this means!' declared the Area Controller for North London. 'In a month, at this rate, there won't be a woman alive in the country, and the

Scourge has reached such dimensions that nothing can stop it leaping to other countries. The whole planet will soon be infested with this virus, or whatever it is, which destroys female life.'

'I still have no answer,' Jeffrey replied dully. 'It is the scientists who must work on it. They are always saying they can create life. Now is their chance.'

'And supposing they fail? If that happens we'll perish. There will finally be only one man left.'

There was silence for a moment, all the grim-faced men waiting for Jeffrey to speak. He looked about him.

'If it comes to that,' he said, 'I shall be that man. The last man on Earth.'

'Why you?' demanded the South London Controller.

'Because I shall live longer than anybody else. I mentioned in my broadcast that I am eternal — if seven thousand years or so can be called eternal.'

'So that's it,' said the North London Controller. 'This potion which has given you the power to be different from all other men has brought about the destruction of women!'

'Unintentionally. Do you think I'd be such an idiot as to deliberately kill all the women in the world? It shatters every scheme I ever had. It makes the future impossible, because without women — '

Jeffrey stopped dead. Mira Sandos, and the world of the future! There had been women there because he'd seen them. Slowly he relaxed in his chair, half smiling to himself.

'You need have no fear, gentlemen,' he said presently. 'Everything will come out all right. Women will remain to populate the Earth.'

'I'd like better proof than just your say-so, Mr. Collins,' one of the men said bitterly. 'I've already lost my two daughters and I may lose my wife. What makes you think she in particular won't be affected as the others have been?'

'I offer no such assurance, I'm afraid. I merely say that in the future women will be present, as they have always been. I don't pretend to know why this should be so. I just . . . know.'

It had suddenly occurred to Jeffrey that nobody knew he had travelled Time — except Betty, and she was dead — so there was nothing to prevent him adding to his power by taking on the mantle of a seer. In the most sophisticated of human beings there is always an element of superstition. It would enhance things immeasurably if he played on this foible.

'How can you be so sure?' asked the North London Controller.

'Because, as you remarked earlier, I am not as other men. To have become almost eternal has also given me other qualities. Call it a psychic gift if you wish.'

'I think you're an infernal liar,' declared the Western Area Controller, and before anyone could stop him he had snatched out the gun with which, officially, he was equipped and fired it point-blank at Jeffrey's chest. A red spot appeared on his white shirt above the heart but his expression did not change.

Certainly he felt the impact of the bullet, and with it a brief and deadly sickness — then the tremendous adaptive force his body had built up reacted and absorbed the shock. He got to his feet slowly and looked at the dumbfounded Controller.

'You are wasting your time.' Jeffrey's voice was measured. 'There is far more to this gift of longevity than you realize. I am in an invulnerable position because I cannot be killed. But you can be; and you shall. That was a deliberate attack on the head of the State.'

Jeffrey jabbed a button on his desk and two of the militia came in. He signalled to them and the Western Controller was seized and bundled out of the office.

If the incident had done nothing else it had shown the rest of the men the kind of problem they were dealing with. They were grimly silent as Jeffrey wiped away the bloodstain from his shirt with his handkerchief, then he eyed them each in turn.

'In the old days, gentlemen,' he said, 'before war tore the world to pieces, a man was judged by the amount of power he possessed. I think I have proven that I have more power than the rest of men, which is sufficient reason why I should rule this country as I see fit — and later, maybe, the world.'

'As your Controllers,' commented the South London man, 'we also should be eternal.'

Jeffrey smiled coldly. 'I think not. I do not intend to share my power with others. And,' he added, as he saw the men glance at each other, 'if you are thinking you will somehow find the formula — steal it maybe — and use it to your own advantage, you had better think again. I have it in one place only, my memory. Get it out of there, if you can!'

The Controllers gradually became more respectful.

'What are we to tell the people, Mr. Collins?' asked the North London man. 'You know the mood they are in if these women's deaths continue there'll be trouble — '

'I'm prepared for that,' Jeffrey interrupted. 'I can do nothing about the deaths. It is up to the scientists to find a counteractive, though I hardly think they will.'

He had nothing more to say than this

so the Controllers had to depart to deal with the people as best they could.

And the Scourge continued relentlessly, a devouring flame throughout the country, felling every living female of no matter what species.

Jeffrey set his face stolidly against the people who vilified him. He clung to the original plan he had made and hoped for some kind of miracle to halt the Scourge, which was now appearing in countries abroad.

Inevitably, by sheer force of circumstance, the men grew slowly accustomed to the disappearance of womankind. At first there had seemed no point in the vast rebuilding schemes which Jeffrey had devised, but by degrees the men realized that they had to live somewhere, even if without families, and so a new London grew out of the ashes.

By 2028 the Four-Year Plan was complete and so was a new metropolis. And the female population of the world had dropped to half. Statistical calculation showed that, according to the number of births still being recorded, the human race had perhaps another century to live. To which observation Jeffrey merely smiled. He had seen for himself that in the future women were present, so was undisturbed. Time could not lie. What had happened must happen again.

By 2030 his position in the world was both unassailable and unique. His various pacts with other countries had manoeuvred him to a pinnacle of extreme power, so much so that his word was becoming increasingly significant. It seemed that before long he would, by virtue of his invulnerable constitution and all but eternal life, come to rule the world. Not that men objected any more to such an idea In most of his schemes he revealed an unusual brilliance and his general tendency seemed to be to help the masses of the people to a more easy form of life — but he was hampered by the lack of womankind. The essential softening influence was absent, and without it, Jeffrey knew, he could never completely assume the position of absolute dominance that he sought.

In 2032, when the Scourge had

accounted for three quarters of the female population, he exhorted the hard-working scientists to find some solution to save the last remnants of femininity — and at the same time withheld the secret of his own formula for fear of losing his own power. This was equivalent to telling the scientists to work blindfolded. Without knowing the formula that had caused the Scourge they could not possibly find an antidote . . . So the women kept on dying.

'It comes to this, Mr. Collins,' the head scientist for London told him bluntly, when summoned to headquarters to report progress. 'We, as biologists and anatomists, cannot possibly save woman-kind unless you tell us the exact ingredients of the potion you gave your wife. When we know that we can probably find something for an antidote.'

'That formula exists only in my memory and I have no intention of divulging it,' Jeffrey answered curtly.

The scientist was a middle-aged, purposeful man who had lost the distaff side of his family in the Scourge, and as a scientist he was completely unafraid of this iron-faced grey-haired man who almost ruled the world.

'You would prefer to destroy the human race?'

'It will not be destroyed. I am confident of that.'

'Because of some future vision you have seen, perhaps?'

Jeffrey swung from the great window that overlooked 2032 London. 'Yes, if you must know. I can see the future.'

'Did you see yourself in this — vision, Mr. Collins?'

Jeffrey did not answer. He hardly knew what to say. Though physically he had been into the future he had not seen himself as he might be in the thousands of years to come. He had heard the Mind, and assumed a great deal.

'Perhaps,' the scientist said slowly, 'your vision was not of this human race, but of some other. People of another world, maybe, settled here, not unlike us in appearance.'

Jeffrey shook his head. 'I do not believe that. Even I know that people of another world could never so completely resemble us as did the people of 7012.'

The head scientist looked surprised. 'Oh? So you even know the year of your vision?'

'Well — yes.' Jeffrey hesitated and looked again through the window whilst he collected his thoughts. Behind him the head scientist stood musing, a slow smile appearing.

'You couldn't,' he said finally. 'No vision could be so absolutely exact as for you to know the year. I'll make one guess. The machine invented by Irwin Whittaker — or supposed to be — and later relegated to the British Museum, was a machine to travel Time. I'll guess further and say that you did travel Time and have kept the fact a secret, preferring this present pose as a seer. Effective with the masses, perhaps, but not with scientists.'

Anger flashed into Jeffrey's face. 'How do you know so much about Irwin Whittaker?'

'Why shouldn't I? The death of Irwin Whittaker and your trial was one of the strangest cases in legal history before the war. I read every detail and I went and looked at that queer machine which had been found in his laboratory. I was a young scientist in those days and even then I could see possibilities about that machine — possibilities I did not dare mention. That machine travelled Time, didn't it?'

Jeffrey was silent.

'I remain convinced of it,' the scientist added. 'And I shall inform the public and so destroy your power as a seer. Wipe out just one fraction of your mysterious hold over the populace and the rest will start to totter as well.'

'Why destroy that?' Jeffrey snapped. 'I have served the people well. My Four-Year Plan has rebuilt the country.'

'I agree. You have done wonders up to a point. But you are also a menace because you withhold the one thing that can probably save the human race. I would be prepared to forget all about this time-travel exploit of yours; I would even neglect to mention that you have no genuine power as a seer — if you let me have the formula I need.'

'No!' Jeffrey replied obstinately. 'That would make it possible for others to become as eternal as I am and I don't want opposition.'

'You would prefer, then, that I slowly pull your eminence to shreds? First reveal that you have travelled Time and are therefore wise before the event — a not very clever accomplishment; and secondly reveal that you will not save womankind in case you yourself find your power challenged.'

'You cannot prove that I travelled Time. You're guessing.'

'True — but I am right, am I not?'

Jeffrey knew better than try and fool a scientist of such wide experience.

'Yes, you're right,' he admitted. 'But you can't prove it.'

The scientist smiled. 'I think I can, Mr. Collins.'

With that he turned aside and Jeffrey watched in surprise as he went over to the big light fitting above the desk. He unscrewed what appeared to be a bulb and brought it across. Now Jeffrey came to look at it he could see it was a highly sensitive microphone made of glass-clear plastic.

'What the devil does this mean?' he demanded, and the scientist shrugged.

'It means, Mr. Collins, that every word of our conversation in here has been recorded, including your admission a moment ago that you have travelled Time. I hardly think I need more conclusive evidence than that, spoken in your own voice.'

It took Jeffrey several seconds to grasp what had happened, then he gripped the scientist's shoulder and shook him violently.

'You mean that you secretly wired that thing up? That you have recording equipment in your lab. taking down all we said?'

'Exactly. I tried every other way to get a hold over you, Mr. Collins, and make you reveal that formula of yours, and I failed. So I resorted to this method. It is up to you now. Either you let me have the formula and try and save what is left of womankind, or I deliberately set out to topple you from your perch.'

Jeffrey's first impulse was to kill the man, but if he did that he would have an angry populace to face. The people knew that the head scientist was working hard on the problem of saving womankind. His sudden demise would never do . . . No, there was only one answer and Jeffrey was wise enough to know it.

'Very well,' he said at length. 'You shall have the formula — and I am relying on your word that you will do nothing to jeopardize my position.'

'You have my assurance. My sole interest is saving the human race.'

'The formula will be in your hands by ten o'clock tonight,' Jeffrey promised.

Satisfied the scientist turned to the door, the microphone in his hand. Then he paused and looked back.

'If you are entertaining ideas about eliminating me, Mr. Collins, I should forget them. Because, if you do that, you in turn will also be eliminated.'

'I cannot be — and you know it.'

'On the contrary. You could not, for instance, survive in your own waste. Were you to be sealed in a room you would die. So you see, even your claim to being virtually eternal carries very little weight.'

The scientist smiled coldly and then added: 'A pity I know so much, isn't it?'

And with that the head scientist left the office. And, in spite of his inner misgivings, Jeffrey kept his word and had the formula delivered at ten o'clock that evening — and from that moment onward he had little peace of mind. He knew that Saunders, the head scientist, was a brilliant man and for that very reason he profoundly distrusted him. He had already shown what he could achieve by subtlety, and there was nothing to stop him performing a similar act again. It all depended on the extent of his ambition.

A week passed and Jeffrey heard no more of the scientists' activities, though indirectly he gathered that they were hard at work on possible antidotes, basing their findings on the formula. Then, in a fortnight, came news — and Saunders himself brought it to Jeffrey's office.

'Success, Mr. Collins!' he announced, putting down the formula on the desk. 'We have experimented on a female white mouse, and more recently upon a woman volunteer. The Scourge is defeated!'

In spite of himself Jeffrey was conscious of a vast relief. He motioned to a chair and the head scientist seated himself.

'So you will not be the last man on Earth, after all,' he said dryly. 'I have made arrangements for the antidote to be flown immediately to all stricken areas and you may rest assured that from here on womankind will cease dying.'

'Excellent news! And what is the antidote?' Jeffrey asked. 'How does it work?'

'You are not a scientist, Mr. Collins, so I doubt if you would understand the intricacies.'

'I think I would. I worked out the details of the original formula so I am surely capable of understanding the antidote?'

'Well — possibly. To put it briefly, the antidote is the formula itself, but with a variation of quantities in the matter of ingredients. A little more of this, a little less of that, and there it is. Based on the principle of a poison mitigating a poison, which is an age-old law of chemistry.'

'I see.' Jeffrey had the feeling that

something was being kept from him, but he did not know what, or why. He still had his distrust of Saunders.

'Our job being accomplished,' Saunders said, getting up. 'The formula is returned to you, Mr. Collins. I assume I may now return to my normal routine?'

'Yes. Yes, of course.' Jeffrey gave a nod and with that the scientist departed.

For a time Jeffrey sat thinking. The formula was no longer his own secret. He felt that something of his power had been taken from him and that Saunders might make more trouble for him.

Then gradually, as week followed week, Jeffrey felt safe again. Saunders was pursuing his normal activity in the city laboratories, and the people were in a happy mood now they realized the Scourge had been arrested. Jeffrey went to the length of proclaiming a public holiday when there came news of the birth of a baby girl for the first time since the Scourge had started.

None of which could give him back Betty. And he still had ideas about a successor to his high office. So he began to look about him. He made no secret of the fact that he would be interested in meeting a woman willing to assume the responsibilities of being his wife.

Saunders, when he heard of this, gave a sardonic smile.

'It might be worth our while to accommodate him,' he told his scientific colleagues. 'Of ourselves we will never be able to penetrate the official barriers with which he surrounds himself, but a woman with whom he believes he is in love could accomplish much. Jeffrey Collins is not scientist enough to be entrusted with the destiny of mankind for seven thousand years to come.'

'Which is why you too made yourself eternal?' one of the scientists asked.

'Exactly. With that formula in my hands I could hardly ignore its enormous possibilities. Only as time goes on will Collins realize — if he is still in existence — that he is not alone in his glory.' Saunders reflected and then added, 'We ourselves stand little chance of uprooting him because he is suspicious of us — but a woman, working under our orders, might do a great deal. It requires very little to put Collins out of the running. Just a phial of the antidote and his longevity will be destroyed, but obviously only somebody intimate with him can administer it.'

The men nodded slowly and looked at each other. Saunders had made it clear on more than one occasion that he meant to take over the high position Jeffrey Collins had won for himself.

5

Death in space

Accordingly there came into the life of Jeffrey the seductive Elfa Cross. She was one of the young women who had been saved from the Scourge and, from Saunders' point of view, had all the essential qualifications to act as an 'agent'. She had grace, beauty, and intelligence. She came into Jeffrey's life — by easily prepared stages — towards the end of 2032 when, the new London completed, the scientists had turned their attention to the resumption of space flight.

An analytical physicist by the name of Denver Cross, who was, for the time being anyway, Elfa's father, requested that the ruler of the country should visit the space-testing grounds to witness the latest development of an entirely new technology that claimed to have rendered rocket-powered space travel as outdated as the horse and buggy.

To which Jeffrey — now a sombre, stern-faced man feeling the weight of responsibility he carried — promptly responded.

But the moment he first set eyes on Elfa Cross the weight seemed to lift. She was standing by the big window of the main laboratory adjoining the testing ground when he first saw her. In other parts of the big scientific area the experts were gathered, conversing amongst themselves.

'Gracious of you to come, Mr. Collins,' Saunders said. 'I am sure you will find it time well spent. This is Dr. Cross and his daughter Elfa.'

Jeffrey nodded, shaking hands perfunctorily with the scientist; then he turned his attention to the girl. Her blue-grey eyes dropped before his intense gaze. The sunlight caught the waves in her thick, honey-coloured hair.

'You will be aware, Mr. Collins,' Cross said, 'that before the Third War broke out space travel had been established using dangerous and expensive liquid fuel rockets?'

Jeffrey turned from his contemplation of Elfa. 'Yes, of course,' he agreed heavily. 'And that system of space travel is no longer being used by any country, including Great Britain — not least because of one of my own edicts,' he added dryly. 'The sheer expense of space travel can no longer be justified in these days of post-war austerity — not when the need for the military development of space no longer applies following the world armistice.'

Cross smiled cynically. 'Even if any government wanted to revive the old system of space travel, I doubt that they could find sufficient surviving scientists and technicians with the knowledge of rocket technology. The old Space Centres and Missile Bases were targeted and pretty well destroyed in the war.'

'And a good thing, too,' Elfa commented, rather surprisingly. 'It was their destruction that hastened the end of the war. Of course,' she added, 'we still have a fair number of the old artificial satellites in orbit, which are still being used for worldwide communication purposes, and — '

'And which,' Cross cut in, 'are in danger of becoming inoperative before much longer, because we can no longer send space crews to maintain them, nor can we launch new ones.' He smiled complacently. 'That is where my revolutionary new system will prove invaluable.'

Jeffrey was interested. 'And what, precisely, *is* this new system? And more particularly, what are the costs of its development? I warn you, Dr. Cross, that I will not sanction any development that costs anything like the billions that rocket travel did.'

'My system is one using magnetic lines of force, not rocket recoil. I have discovered a way to make the myriad magnetic lines of force cross under control. My vessel tries to get from its existing line of force to the next one to bring itself into balance — it tries to fly away from the position it finds itself in when propulsive power is created by the enforced crossing of lines of force. These magnetic lines of force are everywhere, and by sliding from one magnetic force line to another, speeds undreamed of by any rocket-driven vessel can be achieved. My ship uses a small atomic power plant capable of generating the necessary magnetic flux as needed.'

'And the cost of your new system?' Jeffrey questioned sharply.

'Less than a tenth of the cost of conventional spacecraft.'

Jeffrey nodded. 'Excellent. And I take it you have constructed a prototype vessel?'

'We have,' Cross answered, smiling. 'A test space machine is out on the proving ground if you'd care to see it.'

Jeffrey nodded promptly and the scientists began to move towards the door. Elfa Cross lingered a little behind them until Jeffrey caught up with her.

'I suppose, Miss Cross, that such profound mechanics as these are outside your interest?' Jeffrey asked, smiling, as they followed the others.

'On the contrary, Mr. Collins, I've worked beside my father since he restarted his experiments. I have also a First Class Certificate as a stratosphere jet flyer.'

'You have?' Jeffrey took her arm possessively. 'I would never have expected it in so — so feminine a woman.'

He was rewarded by a demure glance, nothing more.

In the centre of the testing-field a space machine stood in its metal cradle, resting at an angle of 45 degrees. To Jeffrey's surprise, he saw that it was disc-shaped, its diameter more than two hundred feet across.

'There it is, Mr. Collins,' Dr. Cross said.

'Looks like one of those imaginary flying saucers from the last century,' Jeffrey commented dubiously.

'It's saucer-shaped because that is the easiest design for sliding from one magnetic force line to another,' Dr. Cross explained. 'It also allows it to be spun when in free space, thus creating a centrifugal gravity at the rim of the craft. I am prepared to demonstrate it if you are willing to make a test flight.'

'Now? In our present clothing?' Jeffrey asked in amazement.

'Certainly. The old space and pressure

suits that were needed in the pre-war days with their dangerous rockets are obsolete with my new designs. We have spacesuits on board of course, but only for emergency use.'

Jeffrey hesitated and then asked another question. 'What tests have you made so far, Dr. Cross? Have you actually flown this craft into outer space?'

'Not yet, but I know it can be done.'

'Doubtless; and whilst I have every respect for your genius I would much prefer first that this machine be proved infallible. You have overlooked that I cannot take needless risks. I am in too responsible a position.'

'Which is every reason why you should make the flight,' Elfa murmured, and Jeffrey gave her a sharp glance. '*I* have made it,' she added, studying him.

'But your father just said — '

'Father said *he* has not been into space, which is correct. I am his test pilot, shall we say, for proving purposes. I have already flown this spacecraft as far as the orbit of the Moon and back. In secret, of course.'

Jeffrey looked about him in surprise and received silent nods of confirmation.

'And since you, Mr. Collins, are known to be a man of immense physical resistance, no harm could befall you,' Cross added.

Jeffrey was silent, the scientists watching him and the girl with one eyebrow elevated questioningly. It was his masculine pride that finally got the better of him. Certainly he could not allow a girl — and particularly Elfa Cross — to regard him as a coward. He knew perfectly well that his excuse concerning his high position had carried little conviction.

'Very well,' he said, shrugging. 'I'll take the risk.'

The scientists nodded and he hoped he did not look afraid. For he definitely was. Even the knowledge that he was almost invulnerable could not outweigh his fear of leaving Earth. It had always been a weakness with him, even with airplanes.

Walking forward he stepped into the cage that would make the ascent to the spacecraft's airlock. Dr. Cross, Elfa, and the scientists joined him and the cage moved quickly up the scaffolding, stopping at the circular opening in the vessel's side where the immensely thick door stood open.

Jeffrey stepped into the control room — kept on a level by a system of gimbals — and looked about him. Never before amidst such a bewildering complication of controls, had he so regretted his lack of scientific knowledge.

'This,' Dr. Cross said seriously, 'is a most solemn moment, Mr. Collins. A new step forward for civilization, You have been endeavouring for some time to bring all countries under your aegis, and you have not succeeded — chiefly, I suggest, because you have not had a strong enough lever with which to enforce your wishes. With space travel at your command you have that lever. The country which offers that automatically rules the world.'

Jeffrey nodded. 'I am fully prepared to explore the possibilities once I am convinced of the vessel's efficiency. Shall we start?'

'By all means.' Dr. Cross signalled to the assembled scientists and one by one they left the control room. Finally only Cross, Elfa, and Jeffrey were left. The girl went to the switchboard, moved a control, and the massive metal airlock shut and locked itself, a sheath of pure rubber sliding into place across it.

'Before we start,' Cross said, moving to a locker, 'you had better drink this. It will settle your nerves and enable you to stand the take-off more easily.'

He poured out a half tumbler of green fluid and handed it over. Then he did the same for Elfa and himself. Before he handed over the girl's glass, however, he hesitated and gave a faint smile.

'Bad luck!' he exclaimed. 'Three glasses from one bottle! That will never do. Worse than three on a match.'

He took the two glasses — his own and the girl's — which he had filled and tipped them down the nearby disposal chute. Then from a second bottle he poured out a second lot of liquid, handing one of the glasses to the girl.

Jeffrey smiled a little at the superstition,

studied the fluid, then raised it to his lips.

'Don't!' Elfa cried abruptly, and he paused in surprise. A look of consternation flashed over Cross's face, his glass half way to his lips.

'Don't?' Jeffrey repeated. 'But — how do you mean?'

'That glass — give it to me.' Elfa's voice was curt as, almost snatching it from him, she threw the contents down the vacuum-operated disposal chute. Swinging back to Jeffrey she said deliberately, 'Had you drunk that, Mr. Collins, you would have lost your claim to eternity.'

Jeffrey's expression slowly changed and hard lights came into his eyes. His gaze pinned the girl steadily.

'Just what do you mean?'

'My daughter has been working very hard,' Dr. Cross put in quickly. 'At times she has the strangest notions. I assure you, Mr. Collins, that — '

'He's lying,' Elfa interrupted. 'Believe me, that is the truth. I'm not his daughter. I'm a paid agent in the employ of Dr. Saunders, the head scientist.'

'I don't think you need explain any more,' Jeffrey said, steel in his voice. 'Thank you, Miss — er — ?'

'My real name is Virginia Fayne. I was an agent during the war and I am genuinely a stratosphere jet pilot.'

'And you do know how to fly this spacecraft?'

'Yes.' The girl's gaze was perfectly frank and, behind her, Dr. Cross stood with his fists clenched.

'Proceed with the flight,' Jeffrey ordered, after a moment or two, and at that the girl looked surprised.

'But surely you wish to confront Saunders? Don't you realize that all this was a deliberate trick to provide a reason for you taking a special fluid? Didn't you notice how Dr. Cross changed the glasses — ?'

'I noticed, but unless this machine is a complete hulk I still wish to see its possibilities. I have a reason,' Jeffrey added, his merciless eyes straying to Cross.

The girl shrugged. 'Very well. I'll do the piloting myself. Please lie down on the pressure-rack there.'

She indicated it, an airbed sunk into the curved metal wall, and Jeffrey moved across to it. He saw that it was equipped with self-locking safety straps.

Virginia Fayne settled in the deep chair before the controls. Dr. Cross gave her a grim glance and then moved to the second pressure-rack and lay down.

'Ready?' Virginia asked.

'Ready,' Jeffrey confirmed; and the girl moved the controls.

Instantly power was transferred from the atomic plant, creating a powerful magnetic flux, and the saucer-shaped craft began to hurtle into the sky like a giant discus.

Springs twanged sharply in Virginia's chair. The pressure-racks containing Cross and Jeffrey compressed themselves, their bodies half buried in them. Jeffrey grimaced with the strain of acceleration, but such was his adaptable constitution he remained conscious as the frightful velocity continued.

The only sound was that of their rushing through the atmosphere, and after rising in pitch it gradually fell as the air became more rarified at higher levels — then after what seemed an agonizing eternity the automatic control, timed to operate when escape velocity had been achieved, came into action.

Suddenly, all weight and strain vanished. Undoing his strap, Jeffrey actually floated for a moment, and then bounced against the metal floor again as softly as a bubble. The girl snapped a series of switches that set the ship spinning, and gradually an approximation of normal gravity returned.

'Centrifugal force,' she explained, as Jeffrey glanced at her. 'Dr. Cross prepared for everything.'

'Almost everything,' Jeffrey corrected, an odd note in his voice. Then looking at the scientist as he undid the strap and got up from the pressure rack he added, 'I compliment you on your genius, Dr. Cross. A pity you didn't have the good sense not to become involved with Saunders.'

'I'd no choice,' Cross replied. 'Saunders is the head scientist and I had more or less to obey his orders.'

Jeffrey did not pursue the topic for the moment. He turned and looked through the rear port as the girl motioned towards it. Out there, filling all the void, was the gigantic Earth edged with its startlingly thin atmospheric ring, and beyond that were the icy stars.

'Wonderful!' Jeffrey murmured. 'I had always imagined something like this, and now I really see it as it is. The Earth as a planet — the planet I shall very soon completely rule.'

'Very soon,' the girl agreed, smiling.

'That depends,' Cross said, and something in his voice made Jeffrey and the girl turn quickly. The scientist was standing a little way behind them, a laser pistol in his hand.

'Thank you for turning your backs,' he continued dryly. 'You overlooked the first law of defence: never let an enemy get behind you. I'm sorry to have to resort to such melodrama but you leave me no alternative. It is two against one so I must protect myself.'

'Against what?' Jeffrey asked deliberately. 'Nobody is threatening you.'

'Not yet,' Cross agreed. 'But I can tell from your tone, Mr. Collins, that you have something in store for me — so forgive me if I anticipate it by striking first. And whatever I do to you I shall also do to this woman, since for a reason best known to herself, she has crossed over to your side. Only goes to show: never trust a woman.'

Jeffrey was silent, a great segment of Earth behind his head through the porthole. Cross tightened his hold on his gun.

'I never expected this about-face,' he said. 'But since the main aim was to destroy your power I cannot see that it signifies by what means it is achieved.'

'Shooting me will prove of little use, even with a laser pistol,' Jeffrey pointed out. 'You should be aware of that.'

'I am. This is merely a deterrent in case Miss Fayne might attempt something. You make it more than obvious, Mr. Collins, that you are interested in Miss Fayne. It would cause you a considerable amount of grief if she were to vanish from the scheme of things. Unlike you, she is not invulnerable — '

Jeffrey did not wait to hear the rest. He hurled himself upon the scientist, but he was a shade too slow. The deadly instrument stabbed a shaft of amber fire and with a scream Virginia whirled sideways, clutching at her shoulder. Helplessly she crumpled to the floor.

Jeffrey glanced at her, aghast — then back to Cross.

'Are you perfectly sure, Collins, that you can survive a weapon as deadly as this?' the scientist asked. 'I imagine there are limits even to your adaptive powers.'

Jeffrey hesitated. There was just the possibility that Cross might be right. It was a chance Jeffrey could not afford to take, having no real guarantee as to how much his body could stand.

'There's a door behind you,' Cross said curtly. 'Open it.'

Turning slowly Jeffrey obeyed. The now opened metal door gave onto a narrow corridor leading around the rim of the ship. Strip lighting was in operation, casting its glow on massive metal stanchions and ladders.

'Just go on walking,' Cross ordered, his gun steady.

Still Jeffrey obeyed, wondering vaguely what was intended. When he came to the bend of the corridor, it opened out into a larger chamber. Cross's voice came again.

'There's a ladder on your left. Climb it. When you reach the trap at the top keep going.'

'Do you think,' Jeffrey asked slowly, 'that I don't know that trap leads to the outside of the ship?'

'I said get up the ladder — or take a risk on the laser gun. It's immaterial to me. I can't think of anything better than that you should step into outer space. In that unthinkable cold and airlessness you'll be finished.'

Jeffrey swung and dived, and the action was so quick that Cross was not fully prepared for it. He tried to press the gun-button but at that instant he received a smashing blow on the jaw, which sent him staggering backwards, the gun flying out of his hand. Jeffrey hurtled after it, grabbed it, then turned it on the scientist as he staggered to his feet.

'Since you seem determined to try human reactions in outer space, Dr. Cross, you can make the experiment yourself,' Jeffrey said. 'Up the ladder — quickly!'

Cross gave a wild look about him, holding his aching jaw, but the gun was trained relentlessly upon him.

'Or else try conclusions with this,' Jeffrey added. 'You wish to be rid of me, apparently. That being so I might as well return the compliment, especially after what you did to Virginia Fayne. Get up that ladder!'

Rather than face the searing death of the laser gun Cross began to claw his way upward until he reached the trap.

Jeffrey kept immediately below him, gun poised. Then when the trap began to move under the pressure of Cross shoulders the scientist made a desperate effort to save himself.

Twisting suddenly on the ladder, and releasing his hold upon it to do so, he lunged down on Jeffrey, clawing savagely at the gun. The position was such that Jeffrey could not fire so he took the other alternative and forced his way upwards, carrying the battling scientist along with him. The trap flew open abruptly under the combined pressure and with a whistling scream the air was sucked out of the chamber into the vacuum of space, carrying both men with it.

Jeffrey released his hold on the scientist and his body shot outwards like a cork from a champagne bottle, twisting and turning, carried with enough impetus from the brief outrush of air to sail beyond the spacecraft's slight attractive field. Jeffrey too would have passed beyond saving had not the toe of his boot caught against the rim of the emergency lock. It gave him the chance to anchor for a moment.

He was dizzy, his lungs bursting, hammers banging in his skull — yet the inconceivable zero of outer space did not for the moment penetrate to his vitals, chiefly because the human body is insulated when in a vacuum and retains its warmth for a considerable time. He twisted around like a swimmer under water and saw great javelins of ice condensed on the airlock where fragments of inner air remained. He jolted and turned, caught at the underside of the rim with his hand, and felt it go dead from frostbite. This brought him within range of the ship's gravity and he passed down to the base of the ladder.

Barely conscious, he lurched down the corridor and found the metal door at the end of it was shut. With what strength he had left he beat against it. There was sensation in one hand but not in the other. The door opened suddenly and he stumbled forward, to fall flat on his face. The door clanged shut again. He slowly began to realize he was breathing once more, his heart hammering fiercely.

Then an arm came behind his neck and his head was raised. Fiery spirit down his throat set him choking and gasping and with an intolerable stinging circulation began to operate again.

'Better?' asked the quiet voice of Virginia Fayne, and she helped him to his feet.

'Yes . . . ' He could not think of anything else to say just then. He was looking at his snow-white right hand from which all sensation had vanished. He was also conscious of blood trickling from his nose.

'Here,' the girl said, and handed him some wadding. He plugged it in his nostrils and then frowned at her.

'The last time I saw you — '

'I recovered,' she said. 'Cross's laser only scored the top of my shoulder. Not the first time I've been burned, but the shock put me out of action for a moment.'

Jeffrey noticed now that her shoulder was heavily bandaged, remnants of her blouse drawn roughly over it. She helped him to a seat and then moved to the control board.

'I saw what happened,' she explained. 'I was at the porthole here when Cross's body went sailing into space. The outward rush of air slammed the passage door and fortunately for me, sealed the air in here. It dropped a little when I brought you in, but it's okay now. I think we'd better get back to Earth. You've had enough demonstration of what this spacecraft can do, I imagine?'

'More than enough.' Jeffrey looked fixedly at his dead right hand.

'That can be cured,' the girl said briefly. 'I've moved around in scientific circles quite a lot, and extreme frostbite is not difficult to cure. You're lucky to be alive.'

'A little while ago I might have doubted that — but not now. My life took on a new meaning when I met you. Even more so when you stepped right out of the enemy camp and came over to my side. I'm left wondering why you did it.'

Virginia smiled a little, gazing out on to the diamond-bright stars.

'Saunders forgot one thing,' she replied. 'He overlooked that a natural emotion can upset the best laid plans. The thing is simply explained, Mr. Collins. I'm in love with you.'

'Usually,' Jeffrey pointed out, 'it is the man who says that.'

'Are you saying it?' the girl asked deliberately.

'With everything I know.' Jeffrey got to

his feet. 'I remember what you said a little while ago when I was looking back at Earth. I said I would rule it all one day — and you confirmed the fact. I couldn't imagine myself doing it now without you to help me.'

Virginia smiled again as he came over to her. For a moment they forgot the void, the onrushing machine, the not-far-away Earth.

She put her arms around his neck and kissed him.

'I am still young, Virginia,' Jeffrey said at length, when their embrace was finished. 'I shall always be young — as I am now. What years there seem to be are those of responsibility.'

'I know you are virtually eternal, Jeff — everybody does.' The girl reflected for a moment and then added, 'But you are not alone in that. Saunders is also eternal.'

Jeffrey compressed his lips. 'It's no surprise. I always thought something like that had happened, ever since I was forced to give him the formula.'

'He is a dangerous enemy. He believes

you unfit to guide the destiny of mankind because you are not a scientist. And since he is as invulnerable as you are I don't see how you can dispose of him.'

'I may not be a scientist, Virginia, but I know one trick which ought to eliminate Saunders completely. He was a fool enough to tell it to me himself.'

Jeffrey turned and looked through the main outlook window onto the Earth. For a moment the thought of Saunders seemed to have gone from his mind.

'Ours!' he murmured, as the girl came to his side. 'Ours, Virginia! Not just mine. You with your intelligence and beauty — and me with my endless life and purpose. We can mould humanity as we will. And reach out beyond that limited Earth to the distant planets. Maybe to the whole Universe, in time.'

'I'll help you as long as I can,' Virginia replied, with a touch of wistfulness.

'As long as you can!' Jeffrey caught at her shoulder with his sound hand. 'Why do you say that? We'll be together — '

'For as long as I live, yes. But only that long. You will outlive me by thousands of years. There can be no eternal life for a woman. Don't forget the Scourge . . . '

Jeffrey was silent, his face troubled. This was a moment when longevity did not seem so attractive. Whatever he loved must perish, and he must go on and on. And yet, at the end of the road, there should be . . . Mira Sandos.

'We must make the most of the time we have together,' he said finally. 'We have so much to do.'

6

Deathbed confession

Piloting the amazing craft expertly, Virginia made the descent through the atmosphere. The manoeuvre was far less dangerous than on pre-war space flights, because she was able to slow the craft right down, and re-enter the atmosphere at such an angle that friction was minimal.

On the journey, at Jeffrey's instruction, she ignored the frantic questioning messages from Saunders and his scientists back at the testing grounds, and maintained radio silence.

At length she reached the English Channel, and skimmed across it at a level low enough to avoid radar detection. She eventually brought the craft down on Salisbury plane, near to what had formerly been a military training base.

Jeffrey was instantly recognized, and

such was his eminence that his orders of secrecy at his return were strictly obeyed by the commanding officer. The spacecraft was moved into a hangar, there to await Jeffrey's further instruction.

Jeffrey placed himself in the hands of doctors and radiologists, and thanks to their skill and instruments the frostbite was overcome and new flesh grafted with the result that Jeffrey soon found his right hand as good as new again. Medical checkup proved him to be otherwise none the worse after his contact with outer space. So he was secretly flown by military helicopter to the outskirts of London with Virginia, where he took over a private hotel. Here, he and Virginia were quietly married, and then made further plans against Saunders.

Saunders himself still did not know whether Jeffrey Collins had returned to Earth. This worried him considerably.

'I just don't understand it,' he declared to his colleagues, when they had gathered together in a private room of the major laboratory to discuss the matter. 'Virginia Fayne ought to have got into contact with us if she came back safely. Instead we get no word from her or Dr. Cross. And the valuable prototype spacecraft has vanished!'

One of the men connected with the astronomical section put in a word. 'The spacecraft made its test okay, sir. We followed it to about halfway to the moon, then it turned and came back again. We lost track of it because it made its re-entry on the other side of the world — and since it was a secret flight no one there was tracking it for us.'

Saunders drummed his fingers impatiently on the bench.

'Only thing I can think is that perhaps Collins saw through the trick somehow, wiped out Virgie and Dr. Cross, and then came back to Earth.' He shook his head. 'No, even that doesn't tie up. Collins doesn't know how to control a spaceship. He could never have flown it home, else it would have crashed. Either Cross or the girl did the piloting, but why don't we hear something?'

Some of the men were surprised that Saunders had such faith in Virginia

Fayne. The fact that she might have about-faced never seemed to occur to him.

'Wherever Collins is, if he has returned to Earth,' one of the scientists said, 'he's keeping remarkably quiet. And that doesn't seem logical since he rules the country. He has no reason to be so inactive.'

'We'll go ahead with our plans,' Saunders decided. 'We will form the Clique we decided upon and put our own rules into force. There is no reason why we cannot make a tremendous profit out of being masters of the country. Later our power can extend over the whole world, chiefly because we have the monopoly of space flight.'

'We hope,' one of the chemists said laconically, and Saunders glanced at him in surprise.

'I mean,' the chemist explained, 'that that spacecraft descended on the other side of the world. Maybe some foreign power is busy right now examining it. If so it isn't our special secret any more.'

'We'll cross that bridge when we come

to it,' Saunders answered. 'Meanwhile if Collins should turn up we'll deal with him. He's already been absent long enough for the public to ask where he is. I'll invent a reasonable excuse to satisfy them.'

With that he brought the meeting to a close and the scientists dispersed to continue with their various occupations. Few of them were deeply concerned with the project on hand, chiefly because they had not the advantages of Saunders. He was the ruling voice in the scientific world and he was also almost eternal. With these attributes he had no need to set limits on his ambitions.

But like all men with great ambitions he lived in a state of constant worry. Not to know whether Jeffrey Collins was dead or alive was a persistent, haunting fear. He did not know but what, at some unexpected moment, Jeffrey might suddenly reappear and exact vengeance — or attempt to — for the trick that had been played upon him.

In a troubled frame of mind Saunders returned to his mid-city home that evening. He was living alone and most of his housework was performed by domestics who visited during the day, and by automatic means. He had a meal and then retired to the room he used as a study to work out the grandiose plans he had for shifting control from Jeffrey Collins to himself.

Once or twice as he worked he glanced up, fancying he caught an unexplained sound; then he continued writing and scheming, the desk light casting most of the room into shadow and etching out his lean features into bleak whiteness.

His imagination had not been playing him tricks, however. There had been sounds, and Jeffrey Collins, with Virginia at his side, had been responsible for them. At the moment he was standing in the garden at the back of the house, studying the bright rectangle where stood the curtained study window.

'Only this to tackle now, Virgie,' he murmured, 'and then I think our friend Saunders is nicely sealed up. Kind of him to tell me that no living creature can survive in its own waste. I don't expect he ever believed he'd be the first to prove it.'

'The door is effectively sealed, anyway,' Virginia said.

For the past half hour he and the girl had been at work, right inside the house, having entered it by carving a hole in the glass of the front door and reaching inside to the catch.

This was no hurried plan they were executing. With them, thanks to the girl's knowledge, they had the necessary equipment for carrying out their task. It was noiseless and powered by powerful batteries. They had silently sprayed the outside of the study door with a synthetic liquid rubber.

Taking only a few seconds to harden it sealed every crack with a core as hard as granite. Every part of the study door, on the outside, was a solid mass of the substance.

The study was electrically heated and had no chimney to block up. The only vantage point in need of sealing was the window.

Jeffrey set the spraying nozzle in position, then signalled the girl to switch on — and immediately the creamy fluid, nothing more than the gentlest haze, struck the window and began to congeal upon it.

Saunders did not hear anything, any more than he would have heard drizzling rain. He worked on steadily, unaware that with every second the last possible air escape in the room was being choked up.

'If he has a gun in his desk he might blast his way out,' Jeffrey said, when the window had vanished behind the solidity. 'We'd better stand by for that though I would prefer him to die in there, mysteriously, inexplicably.'

'I don't think he keeps a gun,' the girl responded. 'I was interviewed by him in that very room when he 'recruited' me, and he opened the desk drawers several times to obtain papers — but I saw no weapon.'

Virginia was correct. Saunders did not possess a gun. He was assured enough to scorn firearms. Particularly so since he had made himself eternal.

'You realize what we've done?' Jeffrey

asked presently, as he and the girl waited under the stars.

'Done? Of course I do! Eliminated the man who tried to kill you. Only you've proved yourself smarter than him!'

'With your help. I don't know what I'd do without you. Had you been Betty — the girl I was married to before the Scourge — you'd have accused me of murder.'

'Murder!' Virginia laughed softly. 'It isn't murder when the stakes are as high as ours. If you wish to have absolute domination you are bound to stamp on those who get in the way.'

Jeffrey was swayed by an odd thought for a moment. Now he had found a woman who thought as he did, whose outlook was just as callous, he was not sure that he liked it.

In fact he was not certain but what he would have preferred to be reviled. It would have made him seem all the more powerful when insisting that he had done right. Strange thoughts, strange speculations. He found himself floundering in the midst of them, to be brought back to awareness suddenly by Virginia's calm voice.

'How long will he take to die, do you think?' Virginia asked.

'Depends on his resistance. It's immense, as mine is.'

'We can wait,' Virginia said, without any change of voice, and Jeffrey glanced at her in the starlight. Her well-cut profile was clear against the grey of the night. There could be no other woman like her, Jeffrey decided. She was without pity, every bit as hard as himself.

And in the meantime Saunders was commencing to feel the effect of lack of air, an ever-increasing carbonic-acid gas. First he began to yawn, then he felt increasingly warm, and at last he got to his feet in irritation as his thoughts became too clouded to focus properly. Going to the door he pulled on it and frowned when it failed to budge . . .

That was the beginning. Half an hour later he was hurling furniture uselessly at the door and blocked-up window, but he might as well have tried to escape from a sealed mausoleum. His strength gave out at last and he collapsed on the carpet. If only the telephone had been in his study instead of in the hall . . . But Virginia, from her previous visits and with her photographic brain, had remembered exactly where it was.

By four in the morning Dr. Saunders was dead.

★ ★ ★

The death of Saunders in a sealed room, and the sudden reappearance of Jeffrey Collins at his normal headquarters in London had a shattering effect on the scientists who had been under Saunders's banner. They were even more alarmed when, two days after Saunders's death, they were summoned to headquarters.

To their surprise Jeffrey was not alone. The woman they had believed on their side was with him, seated at the opposite end of the desk.

'Gentlemen,' Jeffrey said briefly, 'I have need of you, otherwise I would give orders for every one of you to be wiped out for plotting with the late Saunders to encompass my downfall. It happens that I will show you leniency because the new world I am intending from here on to create demands scientists in every field. You are summoned here to learn what I shall require of you, and also to understand that this lady is now my wife. If she gives an order you will obey it.'

The scientists did not speak.

'Any more attempts on my life will be drastically dealt with,' Jeffrey added. 'And now to business . . .'

He kept the scientists at it for over an hour, explaining exactly what he wanted. At first they were interested, then there were murmurs of protest, and finally flat refusal to carry out the instructions.

'This is nothing short of massacre, Mr. Collins!' declared the physicist, who had taken Saunders's place. 'It can't even be graced by the name of 'war' — if there is any grace in such a beastly business. I'll have no part of it.'

Jeffrey eyed him bleakly. 'Mr. Mathison, you know what happens to a soldier who refuses to obey orders?'

'Yes, but this is different — '

'It is not different. You — and all of you — are soldiers even if you are in the scientific background. You'll do as you are told, or suffer the consequences. I am determined to consolidate my position, not only in Britain but all over the world.' Jeffrey's tone changed. 'Frankly, I fail to see your objections to my wife's plan.'

Mathison looked aghast for a moment. 'You — you mean your wife thought of this horrible scheme?'

'I would thank you to be more respectful!' Jeffrey barked.

'I beg your pardon,' Mathison apologized, 'but to me it still seems inhuman to contrive a series of space stations hundreds of miles above every country except this one and then threaten to incinerate the populace with heat-beams created by the sun's rays down to a focus, if the various government heads do not obey. It's too ruthless! No plane can fly that high to defend its own territory, and no country presently has the resources to fire rocket — or any kind — of missiles to take out orbital satellites.'

'Exactly,' Jeffrey conceded. 'Space travel

using magnetic lines of force has given us the monopoly. Afterwards, when they have served their purpose of giving point to my ultimata, the space stations can be used as fuelling or stopping points for outgoing spacecraft. But always, as long as I remain in power, outer space shall be the property of this country.'

'There couldn't be anything more perfect,' Virginia said, smiling. 'Either the people make their rulers do as my husband orders, or else they will be like ants under the rays of a magnifying glass.' She sighed. 'I know science can be very horrible sometimes in order to be effective.'

The scientists looked at her and then at each other. It was beyond them how any woman could have conceived such a plan. Then Mathison frowned.

'Mrs. Collins, is this idea entirely yours?' he asked.

'Entirely.' Her eyes met his in defiant pride. 'I have been a scientist all my life, apart from my brief excursion as an agent.'

'And you propose, according to these

plans, that spacecraft should carry the necessary materials into space for these satellite stations and then erect them so that they carry gigantic crystal lenses capable of bringing the sun's heat radiations to a focus on any given spot on Earth?'

'Why not?' the girl laughed. 'It is just the old stunt of schooldays when you burned your lover's name on a tree.'

'The simile is not very apt,' Mathison said coldly; then he looked at Jeffrey. 'Very well, Mr. Collins, you leave us no choice. We must obey or — be removed.'

'Sensible of you,' Jeffrey commented. 'The original spacecraft in which I made my trip into space is presently concealed in a hangar at the Salisbury plane military base, awaiting my orders to return it. Use it as the model for future spaceships that will do the haulage work. Turn all engineering projects into the task of making the space islands.'

The scientists moved towards the door; then Jeffrey added,

'If you try in any way to impede my plans, gentlemen, or attempt to trade the

186

secret of lines of force space travel to any other country I shall strike you down, and your families also.'

The scientists went out and closed the door. For a while Jeffrey sat musing, then he glanced at Virginia as she laughed softly. Her gentle hand rested on his.

'You just don't know how to use your power,' she said gently. 'I'm no believer in long-winded negotiations and subtle traps. Brute force backed by terrifying scientific power is the only method. I know it so well.'

'Know it so well?' Jeffrey repeated, frowning. 'How do you mean?'

She did not answer the question. Instead she got to her feet. Virginia went round the back of his chair and then put a slender arm about his neck.

'Jeff, are you like that scientist? Shocked that I should think out such an effective way of making other countries listen to you?'

'No, I'm not exactly shocked, but . . .'

'But what?' Her smile had gone for the moment and her blue-grey eyes pinned him. He had never thought they could look so cold, so transparent.

'Well, I still can't quite get over the fact that a woman can think as I do. I know there's a reason for my outlook because I have changed the whole balance of my mentality and emotions; but there is no such change in you. It's surprising, to say the least.'

'The true scientist can't afford to be swayed by sentiment,' she answered. 'Later on I'll think out other schemes to help you. You wanted to be master of the world, and you shall be.'

And by the spring of 2033 practically every country was aware of the departure from Earth of spacecraft, taking with them immense quantities of engineering material. This, once the initial drag of the takeoff had been overcome, was not a difficult task since in space everything became weightless and was easily towed along in the void.

But each country viewed with wonder, and a dawning fear, the telescopic photographs that showed the gradual assembly of enormous space stations, rather like mighty metal globes which sprouted highly polished lenses set on arms at the sides of the spheres.

What did it all mean? Why were these things being put into an orbit that made them incapable of falling back to Earth? Why were they so mathematically timed that they kept pace with Earth's revolution and therefore remained centred over one particular country, at a height so tremendous no airplane could ever reach them?

Jeffrey did not answer any of these questions even though the heads of each country asked him what it all meant since it was obvious that the spacecraft had their takeoff grounds in England. Actually Jeffrey was stalling for time for it would be two more years before the great engineering project he had started could be completed. In the meantime his rulership of the country went on much as before, though there were a few laws that he rigidly tightened up, chiefly at the suggestion of Virginia.

There were even times when he wondered whether he or she were ruling, for she had certainly become the power behind the throne.

By the middle of 2034, however, Virginia had other matters on her mind. She was anticipating the heir whom she intended should carry on Jeffrey's destiny when the time came, provided it proved to be a male child.

Several times during 2034 Jeffrey went out into the void to study progress. By this time he had overcome his fear of space and such was his constitution he was well able to endure the rigours of the take-off. He found that the cosmic engineers had made tremendous advancement. The Spheres as they were popularly called, were small cities in themselves, outposts in space equipped with every conceivable requirement and in touch with Earth by radio-television.

To satisfy the constant inquiries of neighbour countries Jeffrey had put out the story that the space stations were to reflect television and radio transmissions, to replace the aging pre-war satellite systems, and also to examine space more minutely than was possible from Earth. But this did not fool the scientists. Their attention was on the giant lenses and it needed no effort of their mathematical brains to appreciate that if those lenses were at any time unmasked they could easily concentrate solar heat waves down on to Earth. So disquiet grew.

Jeffrey returned to Earth at the close of 2034 after a protracted absence. His first enquiry was for Virginia. Radio information had told him that her child was about to be born prematurely, but by the time Jeffrey reached the hospital the event was over. He'd had a daughter — but the child had been born dead.

Immediately he received the news his expression changed. The surgeon in charge added quickly:

'We did everything to save the baby, but we failed. The complications took us utterly by surprise, and — '

'*Complications!*' Jeffrey shouted, grabbing the surgeon by the shoulders. 'What the hell are you talking about?'

'Your child was born with a new form of the Scourge,' the medico said slowly, gently disengaging Jeffrey's grip, and taking a step back. There was genuine contrition — and not a little fear — in his eyes.

'By the time we had realized it, and worked out an antidote, it was too late to use it: the infant was dead.'

'What about my wife?' Jeffrey demanded. 'Has she also been infected?'

'Yes, along with the midwife attending. We isolated them and administered an antidote. The midwife has made a full recovery, and we believe we have succeeded in stopping the Scourge from spreading again . . . '

He hesitated, as if reluctant to speak. It was obvious that the surgeon was mystified — and frightened of Jeffrey's reaction.

'I don't give a damn about the blasted midwife!' Jeffrey's voice rose in fury. 'What about my *wife*? Will *she* live?'

The surgeon looked distinctly uncomfortable. 'She was already severely weakened by the premature delivery . . . she'd lost a lot of blood. Pending a transfusion, we couldn't administer the antidote at the same time as we could the midwife, and . . . ' his voice trailed off.

'*And what?*' Jeffrey demanded.

'She's dying,' the Surgeon admitted

quietly. 'She's been told — '

'*You incompetent fool!*' Jeffrey snapped, cutting him short. 'I must see my wife — take me to her at once!'

When he reached Virginia's bedside he dismissed the surgeon and stood looking at her. Her eyes were fixed on him and she was smiling faintly.

'I'm sorry about our baby,' she said quietly.

'Never mind that,' Jeffrey said, settling on the side of the bed. 'I've been told you're dying. In God's name — *why*?'

'It's because of your longevity treatment, Jeff,' Virginia whispered. 'Doctor Morrissey explained it to me . . . '

'Morrissey? That fool of a surgeon you mean?'

'He isn't a fool, Jeff. He did all he could. He told me that the intermingling of your DNA with mine in our child — a girl — had created a new form of the Scourge . . . ' she paused, apparently struggling for breath. 'The child gave it to me — and the midwife . . . '

'Who's fine, apparently,' Jeffrey said bitterly. 'But our child is dead — and you

193

as good as! That damned fool Morrissey will pay for this — '

'It wasn't his fault, Jeff: I told you that . . . ' Virginia was breathing very rapidly. Then before she could proceed any further she seemed to suffer some kind of paroxysm which ended in coughing. Jeffrey half rose to fetch the surgeon but the girl detained him.

'You might as well know the truth, Jeff,' she said at last. 'I'll be dead soon, and I want you to know the truth.'

'The truth? What insanity are you talking?' Jeffrey demanded.

'I — I am a Russian,' Virginia explained, after a pause. My real name is Tanya Zharkov . . . I could have kept my secret from you but it's bound to come out after I've gone.'

'Russian? Zharkov?' Jeffrey repeated, stupefied. 'Virgie, you don't know what you're saying!'

'Listen, Jeff, every word is perfectly true. The real Virginia Fayne made many flights, and on one of her spying missions she was shot down over Russia. She was badly smashed up on the landing and our surgeons could not save her . . . But it was discovered that I was very much like her, physically. With cosmetic surgery I could pass for her very easily . . . It was decided I should be an emissary for my country and return to the West as Virginia Fayne. By the use of truth drugs — which she could not resist in her low condition before she died — we extracted all necessary information which was passed on to me. So I took her place.'

'As Elfa Cross?' Jeffrey asked, hardly realizing what he was saying.

'To begin with, yes. Nobody in the West knew I was not the original Virginia. My orders were to thin the other nations of the world as much as possible so as to make it easier for my country to take control with the minimum of effort, since we were ourselves greatly weakened during the last war. In time, it was intended that I would have stolen a new spacecraft and defected to Russia — without you realizing what had happened to me. A way would have been found to fake my death, to allay suspicion . . .'

Jeff sat stunned at these revelations, his

expression of disbelief giving way to a growing rage.

'Now you see why I asked you to make those space stations. If your ultimata to the various countries are not accepted there will be a frightful war, which will decimate entire nations. Russia — knowing I was working for them undercover — would have pretended to meet all your demands, even offered to become an ally, so you would not have attacked us. When I defected with the spacecraft, my people would then have been able to duplicate it. But now that cannot happen.'

Jeffrey sprang up in fury. 'No wonder I could never understand you! No wonder I marvelled at your ruthless outlook. Not being of this country and bent only on our destruction you could afford to be callous. And you had to pick me for a husband! You did all the talking, not me!'

'Even a double-agent is still capable of falling in love,' Virginia whispered. 'I do love you, Jeff, and I always shall. Didn't I help you all I could? I never would have gone through with the original plan, after falling in love with you. You must believe me! Our child is proof of it — '

'Child!' Jeffrey sneered callously. 'A diseased corpse!'

He swung on his heel and strode from the room, slamming the door. He felt as though his whole universe had fallen in pieces. He hit rock bottom an hour later when, in his office, he received a message from the surgeon. Virginia — or Tanya — was dead.

7

Mira Sandos

Not for an instant did Jeffrey reveal the fact that he had been fooled — for that was how he looked upon his association with Tanya Zharkov of Russia. Such was the measure of his bitterness he hardly gave her a thought once the funeral, in full state panoply, was over. The only remembrance of her lay in the amazing conceptions she had put forth — such as the space stations. But one man outside Jeffrey knew the truth and he was not slow to reveal the fact.

About a fortnight after the funeral, during the period when Jeffrey was trying to decide how to map out his future, Dr. Mathison, now the head scientist of London, was shown into the office.

'Well, Mathison?' Jeffrey asked, indicating a seat. 'What is on your mind?'

'Mr. Collins,' Mathison said, 'I'm here

to ask you to call off this plan of your late wife's. I have never approved of it, as I said at first. I still say it's plain massacre.'

Jeffrey was silent. He had been trying for some time to make up his mind about the space stations.

'I know your wife was back of the idea,' Mathison went on, 'but with her influence gone maybe you've changed your mind.'

'Why should I?'

'Because your wife had no reason to have an underlying kinship with the rest of our people. She was a foreign spy — a Russian.'

Jeffrey stared in wonder. 'Who told you?'

'Nobody — though I am glad to have such ready verification. I went into the history of Virginia Fayne when I discovered that your wife had superlative scientific skill and uncommon ruthlessness. Records show that the real Virginia Fayne made many test flights, one of them carrying her over Russia, where she was shot down and crashed. Her subsequent escape from that country and finding her way back to the West was attributed at the time to her remarkable resourcefulness. I also found that the original Virginia was noted for her generosity, most of her hard-earned money being given away to those more in need of it than she was. This did not tie up with the Virginia Fayne you married. I jumped the gap in my speculations when I realized how it was possible for the Russians to have made a switch. Somehow, a Russian calling herself Virginia Fayne had penetrated our government and scientific establishments, and you had become her husband.'

'Yes.' Jeffrey's voice was listless. 'I haven't made the information public and I rely on you to respect my confidence.'

'Upon one condition,' Mathison responded.

'Damn your conditions!' Jeffrey retorted. 'If it comes out that I married a Russian spy there's nothing anybody can do about it.'

'The public,' Mathison said, 'will call it an unholy alliance when it becomes known that it was your wife's idea to have the space stations built so that they can threaten every country but this one. Whatever you may say, Mr. Collins, your unfortunate marriage to a foreign spy can have tremendous repercussions. On the other hand, a good speaker could make you sound like a martyr.'

'I assume you wish to do the talking?'

'I will do so willingly — if you have the space stations modified and use them as communication relays or fuelling and observation posts only. Have the dangerous parts removed. I am referring to the lenses, which have every country up in arms.'

For Jeffrey everything seemed to explode at that moment. Still smarting from the deception 'Virginia Fayne' had played upon him, the death of his child, and now another Saunders-like blackmail from Mathison to try and make him change his course —

'No!' Jeffrey declared flatly, jumping up and slamming his fist on the desk. 'If I keep pandering to every blackmailer who comes into this office I'll never get what I want — world domination.'

Mathison got to his feet, his face grim, and without another word he left the office. Immediately Jeffrey switched on the private circuit of the interphone.

'Forbes?' he asked briefly. 'Dr. Mathison is making himself a nuisance. See that he doesn't get too far.'

'Very well, Mr. Collins.'

For Jeffrey a new way of life had begun at that moment. He had reached a mutational point in his career as a near-eternal man. The last vestiges of normal humanity had been pretty well blasted from him by his wife's deception and Mathison's attempt to make him call off his intended march to power, not to mention the medical curse stopping him from having any progeny. He felt he had been the victim of a vast deception and he blamed all humanity for it.

'Get me the chief engineer of the space stations,' he ordered, snapping another button of his switchboard, and in a moment the chief engineer came through, contacted by short wave at his headquarters in outer space.

'Yes, Mr. Collins?'

'If you need to use the space stations within twenty-four hours for the purposes of the master-plan we arranged, can you do it?'

Brief pause, then: 'I think so, sir, though I had rather hoped you would reconsider your — '

'Your personal hopes are of no interest, chief. Just do as you're told. Instruct all staff to stand by for further orders.'

'Very well, sir.'

Jeffrey switched over into the general microphone and said curtly, 'Clear all waves. I have a world announcement to make.'

In another ten minutes he made it, his transmission station swamping all normal broadcasting bands so that everybody, everywhere, was forced to hear him. He left no doubt of what he intended. Control was to be handed over to him, otherwise the space stations would go into action, their dangerous powers already known to the scientists of every land. He gave no more than three hours for a decision to be made, and in that time the world became very much like an overturned anthill.

Government heads refused to heed

203

such an impertinent demand, so the scientists stepped in with a warning of what was to come. Accordingly humanity scurried for shelter, most of it underground, already prepared by those governments who had foreseen that another, perhaps final war of the most terrifying kind was inevitable.

Dr. Mathison heard the broadcast whilst in his car on the Seventh Traffic Level, and he considered it his duty to rally the populace of London against Jeffrey. But for some reason, which the enigmatic Forbes and his agents could have explained, the power in Dr. Mathison's car failed at a critical moment. In consequence it sailed over the edge of the Seventh Level with the scientist in it and crashed to the metal street three hundred feet below.

For Jeffrey, the three hours passed without any communication, which only served to infuriate him all the more. It took him all his time to keep his patience until the stipulated period had run out, but the instant it had he gave the order to the chief engineer out in space — and that commenced the most one-sided, brutal attack on undefended countries in the history of the world.

From the sky, striking down even through clouds, there descended the incinerating beams of the sun itself, brought into fine focus. Stone and metal melted into liquid under the inconceivable heat and wherever a luckless human chanced to be caught he or she vanished like a moth in a carbon arc . . . This could in no sense be called war. It had the incarnate fiendishness of super-science behind it. Jeffrey himself no longer cared what happened as long as he achieved his objective — which he did in a remarkably short space of time.

No air force commander could ask his men to fight a thing like this. No plane could grapple with it, and to blast Britain with H-bombs in reprisal, dropped from planes, would not stop the merciless rays probing from outer space. There was only one thing to do — capitulate, unconditionally. And so, by a monstrous irony, Jeffrey Collins became master of the world on Christmas Day, 3034.

Absolutely alone in his power — for even those who served him secretly hated him — he began in 2035 to lay his plans for the development of the world under his rule for thousands of years to come. He knew he could constantly tighten his hold, for as the existing generation died out the new one could be forced from birth to pay respectful homage to him. He was determined that it should. He had become an egomaniac, lost to everything except the acquisition of more power. He was an immeasurably powerful man, and without a friend.

Years fled by. Because he knew the people hated him he tightened up the rules and regulations day by day until his iron control was absolute around the world. And even here he could not rest.

His eyes began to look beyond the circle of inner worlds — all of them now colonized — to the ponderous giants beyond the Asteroid Belt.

Such was his mistake. He never looked on the ground, on the world from which he ruled. He never noticed the gathering hatred of the people for his domination.

Yet at the moment revolt was impossible for a number of men and women were wholeheartedly behind Jeffrey, chiefly because they had powerful positions and wealth. These were the Faithful, and they saw to it that the masses were quelled on every planet.

2055 moved on to 2065 and in that time Jeffrey had almost forgotten 'Virginia Fayne', or at least the hurt was not as intense as it had been. He still wanted a successor to his power, and so he had instructed medical scientists to find a cure for the development of the Scourge in his children. But so far he had not met a woman who appealed to his utterly unsentimental nature.

The ten years had also been filled with considerable scientific achievements. In consequence Earth now possessed many new amenities — weather control, cold light, and pure synthesis of matter, to mention only a few things. The space stations that had brought the world to its knees were used as deterrents to revolutionaries, and also for thawing out the frozen regions of Earth. By the year 3005 the. Arctic and Antarctic regions literally 'blossomed as the rose'.

Gradually, as he consolidated his power over the colonized planets, the outer worlds still remaining to be conquered, Jeffrey forced the populations of Earth, Venus, and Mars into the category of slaves. They worked for the expansion of Jeffrey Collins's dominion. With every year he became more versed in scientific things, and with every year he became more lonely. The men and women who worked around him were becoming older all the time, yet he remained at the apparent age of the mid-thirties, only his grey hair and a heavily lined face making him seem a good deal older.

In twenty more years, the year 2085, all the faces of his original supporters had vanished and younger ones had taken their place. They too seemed to rapidly grow old and left Jeffrey pondering on the evanescence of man's span upon the Earth. Yet, deep down, he envied them. But for one thing he could even have wished to follow them into extinction, and that one thing was a beacon still thousands of years ahead ... Mira Sandos!

In the year 2095 he launched his invasion towards the outer planets and for nearly ten years his legions of explorers were kept busy constructing habitable domes on the larger of the frozen satellites of Jupiter. Though the isolated colonists were not very useful from a slave point of view, their mining operations certainly were, since the moons were rich in minerals practically non-existent on Earth. With these minerals the power of weapons could be greatly increased and so the onward sweep could go on — and on.

To what end? Jeffrey did not know. He only realized that he must accomplish and never remain still. The years between had to be endured somehow until he arrived at the period where Mira Sandos came into the scheme of things.

In 4005, a thousand years after the colonization of Jupiter's moons, Jeffrey still looked the same man, except that in his eyes there was unutterable boredom. Everything he had ever known in relation to his own time had vanished. The city of London covered nearly all England and was the ruling city of the world, and indeed the whole Solar System. New generations that had sprung up had never known anything else but subservience to the inconceivably wealthy man whose power was such that none dared speak against him.

Jeffrey knew something else now, too. He felt he had reached a milestone in his weird destiny. For his now vast grasp of things scientific and the accumulated wisdom of the years had earned him a single title . . . the Mind.

* * *

To Jeffrey himself the extent of Time seemed frightening, yet his fear that another man might oust him was so intense he never made any other man eternal in order to have a companion. Ever and again a woman drifted into his orbit. If he liked her sufficiently his eminence was such that marriage was more or less compulsory, but every time the fates cheated him. Advances in medical science had led to a cure to prevent the Scourge from developing in his unborn children, but there was still a price. He never had a male successor, and he watched daughters grow and flourish around him, proud of their relationship to the master of the world and the System, for by this time all the planets were ruled by the Mind, and he had his eyes on the greater deeps, those vast unexplored areas beyond the First Galaxy where no space explorer had ever dared to venture.

In the year 6005 the aspect of the world was very much as Jeffrey had seen it in his fantastic time-flight from 2012. He had 907 years still to live before he came to the period when he must meet Mira Sandos, always providing that he would be the Mind at that period. Certainly he could not see how anybody else could assume his mantle.

As the years went by he now and again made medical tests of himself, but there was no sign yet of the age-neutraliser beginning to lose its efficiency. In some ways he was sorry; in others glad.

The 907 years seemed a trifle after the thousands he had already endured. He had arrived at the year 6975 with only 37 years to go before he crossed the point in Time he had once visited. He began to hear of certain familiar people and places. Arlin Jag, an up-and-coming lawyer for instance. Across the mighty street from his headquarters there stood the Temple of Justice, and not far away the Hall of Records. Yes, everything was fitting into place.

He knew something now, also, which had puzzled him thousands of years before — the reason why people had stared at him on that day when he had come out of Time. He must have looked exactly like the Mind, only younger. The bewilderment and sudden retreat from him was no longer a mystery.

That 37 years became 27 and Jeffrey became aware of a great impending change in himself. Analytical tests revealed that ketabolism was returning to him. Cells were commencing to break down. The first signs of his vast age were appearing.

He wondered if his prolonged extension of life would cause him to suddenly collapse, or whether it would be a slow, anguishing process towards inevitable doom. For a time he was alarmed that he might die before meeting Mira Sandos, then he realized this could not be because Time had already shown that she was alive when he was. Providing — always providing — that he was the Mind before whom she had been — and would be — brought. So he lived on through the dwindling years and watched himself losing his grip on eternity. He was so preoccupied with himself that he failed to notice certain changes amongst the people, until — when 27 more years had passed — he was visited by the Controller for London.

'I have to have your instructions, Supreme One,' the Controller said. 'For the first time in your wise rule there are signs of revolution.'

'There are always signs of revolution,' answered the grey-haired, grey-faced man at the desk.

'True, Supreme One, but none so

evident as these. I have investigated, and it seems that for some years now everything has been deliberately organised to overthrow you. The masses are weary of your domination and wish to exert their own individualities. They do not believe that, because you are eternal, they should work only for the extension of your power.'

'Behind such a movement there must be a mastermind,' Jeffrey said deliberately. 'Have you traced such a person?'

'Yes, Supreme One. Surprisingly, it is a woman. Gifted, intelligent, and descended from a race of scientists. I think she is a real danger.'

'And her name is Mira Sandos?' Jeffrey asked, with a glance at the calendar.

The Controller bowed. 'The Supreme One knows all things.'

'Arrest her on a charge of treason,' Jeffrey ordered. 'I will question her in the Temple of Justice.'

'So be it, Supreme One.'

Jeffrey watched the Controller depart and then he frowned to himself. He had not really intended to order an arrest: it had almost been said for him. Time had already written what must happen and nothing of his devising could alter it.

And so he came to the day and the hour when he took his seat amongst the Elders of the Ruling Clique and gazed about him on the serried rows assembled in the Temple of Justice. It gave him a queer feeling to think that beyond a shadowed alcove to his right he ought to be a lurking visitor out of Time, just beyond seeing himself across the barrier of years. Or was Nature so interwoven into a mathematical puzzle that her laws denied the possibility of two men seeing each other as one man for even an instant?

Jeffrey did not know. Here he was up against the unknown factor in the Time problem. Instead he turned his attention to the woman being led into view by the guards.

Yes, it was she! Lightly clad, her hair the colour of rich copper, her features emphasizing perfection. From his high perch Jeffrey drank in her beauty. It had been worth living the thousands of years to have such a woman completely in his power. By union with her he might at last find the successor he so desperately craved.

'Mira Sandos . . . ' Jeffrey began speaking. 'You stand accused before your ruler and his dignitaries of high treason. What have you to say?'

There was silence for a moment and Jeffrey remembered that when he had come out of Time he had heard Mira Sandos just commencing to answer the charge when he had slipped out of the Temple. Now perhaps he would hear what she really had said.

'I have this to say, Supreme One. I admit my guilt in every particular and do not regret one single action that I have performed in my endeavours to release the people from your inhuman bondage. For thousands of years you have held the men and women of this planet and the neighbour worlds in subjection to your own senseless greed. That I have failed in my efforts and will die because of it is of no consequence because I have sown the seeds of a revolution which in a few years will level you in the dust.'

As the girl finished speaking there was a murmuring amongst the people and the dignitaries looked at each other in amazement. Never in the history of the Temple of Justice had any prisoner dared to be so outspoken. Jeffrey himself did not say anything. He was peering across the great space, wondering what colour the girl's eyes were. He was in a particularly difficult position. The desperate love he had for the girl, a love that had hurled him across the ages, was such that he dare not now mention it. If he did his impartial position as ruler would be gone forever.

A dignitary on his right nudged him. 'The Court grows restive, Supreme One. It is for you to speak and condemn this creature. She has dared to plot against you, and admits it openly.'

'Yes . . . Yes, of course.' Jeffrey straightened up. 'Mira Sandos, in view of the extraordinary statement you have just made I do not feel, in the interests of justice, that I can pass sentence immediately. I would prefer to speak to you in my own chamber. Remove — '

'You can't do that!' whispered the man on the right.

Jeffrey glared. 'You dare question my authority?'

'That, Supreme One, has nothing to do with it. Though you are the ruler we are responsible for the decisions that are taken. You cannot hold that against me since you made the order yourself.'

Jeffrey compressed his lips and looked down again towards Mira Sandos. She was gazing at him steadily, the absolute perfection of young womanhood, defiance in every line of her superb figure.

'Speak! Condemn her!' breathed the man on the left.

'And quickly!' added the man on the right — for never before had the Supreme One taken so long to make a decision, and never before had a prisoner been so palpably guilty.

'I refuse to condemn this woman,' Jeffrey said suddenly, leaping to his feet. 'I am the law: I rule every world in the Solar System, and I shall always make the decisions. I repeat my statement: I shall not condemn this woman!'

Aghast silence; then from one of the dignitaries: '*Why?*'

'Because she is right! For untold centuries I have held men and women in subjection. I have been afraid to lose my power. I have been afraid of everything — even of myself! But there must come a time when the breaking point is reached, and that time is now. For thousands of years I have carried the colossal responsibility of ruler, with only one aim — that I might live long enough, and be powerful enough, to come face to face with the one living being strong enough to defy me! That being is Mira Sandos! For the rest of you I have nothing but the utmost contempt. I have crushed you with superlative ease — but here in this woman, still so young, there is a defiance that restores my faith in mankind. She has shown that the spirit of freedom still exists, and is prepared to die for it. For that I refuse to condemn her . . . Give this woman her freedom!'

'What!' shrieked the man on the right, livid. 'Supreme One, you cannot possibly — '

'Give her freedom!' Jeffrey shouted.

The guards did not move. The man on the left jumped up, his position secure only as long as the Supreme One ran true to type. But now he had stepped out of line.

'If this woman goes free she will destroy all that you have built up!' he cried. 'The masses will take control. They will put Mira Sandos at the head and you, all of us, will be swept out of existence.'

'In the destiny of a living race change is essential,' Jeffrey retorted. 'I refuse to pass sentence on this woman. Do as you will.'

He turned away angrily and strode from the midst of his astounded contemporaries. Blurred with fury and inexplicable emotions he reached his private chamber off the main corridor and went within, slamming the door on the sound of confused murmuring that followed him from the Temple's main hall.

Going to the window he sat down heavily and dropped his head onto his hands. He had no idea how long he sat there, fighting with himself, but presently he was stirred to alertness again by the click of the door latch.

He turned sharply as the door closed. Mira Sandos was standing there, the chains removed from her wrists, her clear blue eyes looking at him fixedly.

'Mira Sandos,' he whispered, getting to his feet. 'Then they obeyed the order and released you?'

She shook her head and the light caught the copper waves in her hair. Coming forward she studied Jeffrey intently.

'Your contemporaries did their best to have me returned to the cells for the death sentence,' she responded, 'but the assembled people would not allow it. It was they who released me — the great masses who are behind me. They destroyed your contemporaries, but they will not destroy you. My people are just. They will remember that you refused to condemn me. But of course they will also remember the thousands of years you have exercised a merciless domination.'

Jeffrey did not speak. He was drinking in the beauty of the girl. First it had been a vision seen across Time, the merest glimpse, which had impelled him upon his fantastic course. Yet it had been worth it. She was lovely, soft-spoken, with gentleness in every movement.

'I know why you released me,' she said.

'That is not possible, Mira Sandos. You have not the power to read thoughts, any more than I have, though I do claim to be above the normal person.'

'You are not above the normal, because you are capable of falling in love. You fell in love with me thousands of years ago when a machine crossed Time, and for that you have flogged yourself through the centuries, stamped upon human beings, conquered worlds — all with the intention of giving them to me. In that you are no different from thousands of other men who are willing to give their all to gain the woman they desire.'

Jeffrey could not resist the impulse to grip the girl's shoulders, and she made no attempt to draw away.

'How do you know?' he asked slowly.

'How can you know?'

'Because I can read thoughts. You have forgotten one thing, Supreme One. In thousands of years of evolution human beings develop their brains. In your day, the Twenty First Century, telepathy was an art that was just being discovered. You have not developed it because you have not evolved naturally: you have merely prolonged your original state. With other human beings, born and developing in the ordinary way, coupled with interplanetary travel and the free radiations of space causing mutations, evolution has followed normal lines. Natural telepathic power is possessed by many, and I am one of them. I know everything about you. Everything.'

'Which means,' Jeffrey said slowly, dropping his hands from her shoulders, 'that you are greater than I am.'

'Yes,' she agreed simply.

Jeffrey moved to the window again and looked out upon the city. He felt indescribably tired. Old.

'For this I have crossed thousands of years,' he muttered. 'I never realized that development would go on and that it is I who have been standing still. I am still back in 2012 but have acquired a lot of knowledge. Others have evolved thousands of years ahead. A grim, strange odyssey, Mira Sandos.'

'Your one desire has been to marry me in the hope that there might be a successor to your domination.' The girl's voice was still quiet. 'That cannot be because your domination ended when you refused to condemn me. I have stepped into your place. I am the successor!'

Jeffrey turned slowly, amazement in his eyes. 'Why — of course you are! A successor, yet without any union between us. What kind of a Fate is it that permits a man to come within grasping distance of the one thing he wants only to lose it?'

'Have you asked yourself if you are worthy of reward?' the girl queried. 'The years are strewn with the dead sacrificed to your ambition. You cannot expect to have the one thing you want with a past like yours.'

Jeffrey sighed. If only he did not feel so incredibly tired!

'I have found you, and lost you,' he said. 'Out of the fact that you are my successor I can perhaps extract some consolation, bitter though it is. Positions are reversed. It is no longer for me to say what shall be done to you, but for you to say what shall be done to me.'

'I have no need to pass judgment,' Mira Sandos replied. 'Nature is doing it for you at this moment. Look at yourself, Supreme One.'

She turned to the wall mirror, unhooked it, and handed it over. Jeffrey looked at his face in horrified wonder. It was grey as putty, and in it were traced a myriad lines growing gradually deeper. The thousands of years were commencing to make themselves noticeable as ketabolism returned to him like a consuming flame.

Mira Sandos looked upon the unguessably old man and smiled in sympathy.

'Poor Jeffrey Collins!' She shook her head. 'You planned for so much and gained so little. Greatness does not come from ruthless persistency, but from gentleness and gratitude. That I have learned. And upon those lines I shall try and model this mighty civilization which you have built up.'

Jeffrey could not answer. Age, relentless, was streaming through him. The anteroom was blurring . . .

Mira Sandos stood motionless, erect as a queen in the golden gossamer garment she wore. In silent pity she surveyed the man upon whom clothes now clung in bagging folds, from whom the hair had gone to leave a wrinkled bald pate. His hands changed to claws, his mouth became toothless.

And the returned power of ketabolism and the restoration of the power of nature did not end there. He shrank. He became more wizened. He was not nothing but lines, creases and folds. One thousand, two thousand, three thousand years . . . An outraged nature was taking revenge.

At last the process was finished. Mira Sandos stirred a little and looked at the clothes lying on the floor. She sighed and the faint, pitying smile returned to her lips. Then she crossed to the huge window and opened it, to the sound of cheering in the streets below. She went out onto the balcony and raised her rounded arms in adulation.

'Mira Sandos!' came a mighty roar from the great assembly. 'Mira Sandos . . .'

She threw kisses and behind her a brown dust stirred in the gentle wind.

* * *

Mira Sandos faded out of Jeffrey's dimming vision and, for some reason, she looked suddenly like Betty. Surely it was Betty with her dark hair and round, comfort-loving face.

'I said you can buy another car and have plenty left over,' Betty said. 'Takes you long enough to answer, doesn't it?'

Jeffrey gave a little start and then shook himself. He got to his feet.

'Sorry, Bet. Just doing a bit of thinking — sort of lost myself.'

'Thinking? About what?'

'Whittaker chiefly. I covered quite a lot of ground in those few moments.'

'No use thinking about him, is it? When he paid his cheque you kissed goodbye to everything connected with that car of yours. Or are you wondering about that man you picked up? The one whom you say vanished?'

'I'm wondering about lots of things,' Jeffrey replied absently. 'I'm wondering about time and space, destiny and prediction. I begin to think I've had a glimpse of the future. Some people do now and again, you know.'

'Glimpse of the future? Go on with you!'

'I'm going to put it to the test,' Jeffrey decided. 'Not just at present, but in about a fortnight's time. I intend to call on Dr. Whittaker, and if his opening words are what I think they'll be I'll know then that the fates have given me a chance to see future events.'

Betty's expression was one that came very close to contempt; but nevertheless Jeffrey put his intention into effect and, a fortnight later, duly called on Whittaker.

'Come into the laboratory,' Whittaker invited. 'I'm busy.'

Jeffrey knew then. Whatever he did, no matter what struggle he made, he could not alter in the slightest degree the path he must now take. In his mind he had seen it all happen, and inevitably it must come to pass.

THE END

MIRACLE MAN
THE MULTI-MAN
THE RED INSECTS
THE GOLD OF AKADA
RETURN TO AKADA

We do hope that you have enjoyed reading this large print book.

Did you know that all of our titles are available for purchase?

We publish a wide range of high quality large print books including:
Romances, Mysteries, Classics
General Fiction
Non Fiction and Westerns

Special interest titles available in large print are:
The Little Oxford Dictionary
Music Book, Song Book
Hymn Book, Service Book

Also available from us courtesy of Oxford University Press:
Young Readers' Dictionary
(large print edition)
Young Readers' Thesaurus
(large print edition)

For further information or a free brochure, please contact us at:
Ulverscroft Large Print Books Ltd.,
The Green, Bradgate Road, Anstey,
Leicester, LE7 7FU, England.
Tel: (00 44) **0116 236 4325**
Fax: (00 44) **0116 234 0205**

THE GOLD OF AKADA

John Russell Fearn

When Harry Perrivale wanted to find the legendary lost city of Akada, his expedition to the African jungle included his native bearers, his wife Rita and trader Caleb Moon. But Harry faced mortal danger as Moon had his own dark plans for the treasures of Akada. Then they confronted a mysterious giant white man, who spoke only in a native tribal tongue. His identity and the reason for his jungle upbringing would only be discovered after tragedy struck . . .